'I can't believe I listened to you. I trusted you—'

Caspar took one step towards her, closing the small gap that separated them. In an instant his head dipped down and he pressed his lips to hers. The rest of her sentence disappeared into his kiss.

Caspar St Claire was kissing her!

Involuntarily Annie closed her eyes as his mouth covered hers. His lips were warm and soft but his kiss was far from gentle. It was demanding and insistent and powerful and it made her insides tremble. It was firm enough to take her breath away and make her swallow her words. His five o'clock shadow was rough against her cheek, but even that sensation was pleasant. She should protest, she should resist, but he wasn't giving her a chance and she didn't really want him to stop. For a moment she even thought about kissing him back...

Emily Forbes began her writing life as a partnership between two sisters who are both passionate bibliophiles. As a team, 'Emily' had ten books published, and one of her proudest moments was when her tenth book was nominated for the 2010 Australian Romantic Book of the Year Award.

While Emily's love of writing remains as strong as ever, the demands of life with young families have recently made it difficult to work on stories together. But rather than give up her dream Emily now writes solo. The challenges may be different, but the reward of having a book published is still as sweet as ever.

Whether as a team or as an individual, Emily hopes to keep bringing stories to her readers. Her inspiration comes from everywhere, and stories she hears while travelling, at mothers' lunches, in the media and in her other career as a physiotherapist all get embellished with a large dose of imagination until they develop a life of their own.

If you would like to get in touch with Emily you can e-mail her at emilyforbes@internode.on.net

Recent titles by the same author:

These books are also available in eBook format from www.millsandboon.co.uk

DARING TO DATE
DR CELEBRITY

BY
EMILY FORBES

MILLS
BOON

First published in Great Britain 2013
by Mills & Boon, an imprint of Harlequin (UK) Limited,
Large Print edition 2014
Eton House, 18-24 Paradise Road,
Richmond, Surrey, TW9 1SR

© 2013 Emily Forbes

ISBN: 978 0 263 23858 7

Harlequin (UK) Limited's policy is to use papers that are natural, renewable and recyclable products and made from wood grown in sustainable forests. The logging and manufacturing processes conform to the legal environmental regulations of the country of origin.

Printed and bound in Great Britain
by CPI Antony Rowe, Chippenham, Wiltshire

Dear Reader

I'd like to introduce you to Caspar St Claire, Paediatrician and the star of a reality medical television series. This story began with the idea of Caspar, with his curly, dark hair and mesmerising green eyes he took up residence in my head and refused to leave until I gave him a voice.

Things fell into place from there as he created his story. Despite his celebrity status he was first and foremost a doctor with a very gentle nature so I decided he would suit paediatrics. He also struck me very much as a white knight and therefore he needed a woman. Annie Simpson is that woman.

Their story is ultimately quite different to what I had initially imagined, my characters do seem to like taking over, but in this case I was happy to let them take the lead as they seemed to know what they were doing ☺.

I hope you enjoy a glimpse of country South Australia as Caspar and Annie find their Happily Ever After.

Love, Emily

For my gorgeous Goddaughter, Kate,
I am enjoying watching you grow into a
beautiful woman. Your constant smile
brings happiness to everyone around you
and that is a gift I hope you never lose.

With love and best wishes for a happy life,

Your Godmother.

CHAPTER ONE

'ARE YOU TELLING us or asking us?' Annie demanded.

The rest of the staff who were assembled around the boardroom table seemed to be sitting in quiet acceptance but Annie Simpson wasn't having a bar of that. She stared at Patrick Hammond. Was he serious? Was the hospital director really telling her, telling them all, that Blue Lake Hospital was going to be the setting for a reality television show? That there were plans to film a hospital drama featuring real patients and real doctors, *their* patients and *their* doctors, in *their* hospital, and he expected the staff to get on board?

'I'm telling you what's happening and asking if you're prepared to be part of it.' For a large man Patrick was very softly spoken and today was no exception. If Annie's question had irritated him he showed no signs of annoyance.

Annie knew Patrick didn't run his hospital like a dictatorship—most decisions were discussed with senior staff to some degree. Most *medical* decisions, she qualified. The day-to-day running of the hospital was not something Patrick would normally converse with them about. Annie wondered exactly where a reality television show fitted into the scheme of things.

'Do we have a choice?' she asked.

Patrick rubbed one hand over his closely cropped hair. 'Of course you do. But I would like you to consider what this means for the hospital—money going into the coffers, good publicity, *free* publicity. With so many country hospitals struggling to stay open, having this sort of media buzz can only be a good thing.'

'Are you sure?' Annie argued. 'What if something goes wrong? What if there's a disaster and the hospital gets sued? That won't garner good publicity. And it's not likely the government would close this hospital. We may be rural but we're not a small six-bed outfit. We are a specialist facility in the state's second-biggest town. There would be an outcry if they even mentioned shutting us down.'

'We may be a large hospital but we're still government funded and that means we have the same funding issues as everyone else,' Patrick countered. 'Do you have any idea how many people watched the last series of *RPE*?'

Annie had thought his question was rhetorical but when Patrick paused, obviously waiting for her answer, she shook her head. She didn't have a clue.

'Two million. Every night.'

That was a huge audience for Australian television. Annie had known *RPE*, the series filmed at the Royal Prince Edward Hospital in Melbourne, was popular, but she hadn't realised how popular.

'And Caspar St Claire is one of the stars,' Patrick continued. 'This spin-off series is a big deal. He's a local boy made good. There will be big interest in what he does, not just locally but around the country. And the television network is compensating us nicely for the opportunity to film here.'

'So it's all about the money?'

Patrick shook his head. 'Don't be too quick to criticise, there's a long list of things the hospital needs and the money from the network will go a long way towards providing those things, including refitting a birthing unit for your department. And you do realise Caspar is a paediatrician?' he queried. 'As an obstetrician, I thought you'd be pleased to know that I've found someone to cover Paediatrics while Phil is on long service leave.'

Annie wasn't ready to let Patrick have the last word. She'd been the subject of media interest before and it hadn't been a positive experience. She'd moved to this quiet, regional centre to rebuild her life and she wasn't happy to find that she might be cast back into the public eye whether she liked it or not. Not happy at all. 'I would be pleased if I thought you'd found a replacement who has come to work but it seems to me you've just found one who is coming accompanied by his own circus. I'm not interested in being a part of that.'

'I have never worked with a circus. Children, yes, animals, no, and definitely not circuses.'

Annie jumped as a deep masculine voice spoke up behind her and ran like molten lava down her spine. From the seat beside her she heard Tori Williams, one of the anaesthetists, catch her breath and then sigh, and Annie didn't need to turn her head to know that Caspar St Claire was standing behind her and had obviously heard her every word. She could feel his scrutiny just as she could feel the eyes of everyone else in the room. They were watching her, waiting with interest to see what she was going to do.

She had no idea what Caspar St Claire was thinking and she didn't want to turn round to read the expression on his face, but he had addressed her and she couldn't sit there pretending to be deaf. She turned in her seat to find the devil himself watching her. A rather handsome devil, she had to admit, but that didn't change the fact that she didn't want him here.

Of course, she recognised him immediately. No introduction was necessary, at least from her side. Patrick was right, *RPE* was a huge ratings winner and, even if Annie hadn't actually been glued to her television like everyone else for the last season, she'd certainly caught a few episodes and knew who Caspar St Claire was. But why did he have to turn up here?

'Let me assure you,' he said in his ridiculously rich, made-for-radio voice, 'that my patients always come first and the crew are exceptionally good at being as unobtrusive as possible.'

She wanted to laugh at him. If he thought she believed that for one second he was in for a surprise, but the force of his gaze made the laughter catch in her throat. His green eyes held hers, challenging her to argue with him, but she was temporarily struck dumb. She wished the floor would open up beneath her feet, but of course she wouldn't have the good fortune for that to happen.

Every medical television show had a resident heart-throb doctor and even though *RPE* was a reality show they'd still managed to find some attractive stars, and Dr St Claire was the pick of the bunch. But she hadn't expected him to be even better looking in real life. His dark hair was probably an inch longer than it needed to be but that extra inch gave enough length to let his hair curl, lending him a youthful look. A just-tumbled-out-of-bed look.

As she pictured him tangled up in his sheets, running his fingers through his hair to try to tame it ready for the day, she could feel the heat of his gaze burn into her as he continued to watch her, waiting for her reply. She felt her cheeks begin to flush as her temperature rose but she couldn't think of anything to say.

'Do you have any other objections, Dr Simpson?'

He knew who she was? That shocked her out of her imaginings and back into the real world. Back to reality.

She frowned. How the hell did he know her name?

But she'd have to worry about that later. The rest of the staff was sitting mutely around the table, all watching the interaction, one-sided though it was at present, and there were more important things to worry about than how he knew her name. Far more important things.

'I'm sure I have a lot more objections, Dr St Claire, and without more information, a lot more information,' she stressed, 'I won't make a decision about my involvement. When do you begin filming?'

'Tomorrow.'

Annie's eyebrows shot skywards. She needed more time. She wasn't ready for her department to be invaded by cameras. She wasn't ready for that exposure. Not again. Not by a long way.

The easiest thing would be to say no immediately. To tell him she *didn't* want to be part of this. Then she wouldn't have to worry about anything further. She wouldn't need to wait for more information. There was no way she was going to agree to a media circus in her delivery suites and she should tell him that right now.

She opened her mouth but before she could speak Caspar interrupted.

'Don't say no just yet.'

Annie stared at him. Was she that easy to read? Although she supposed it was a reasonable guess, given her reaction so far. She was tempted to deny her intentions, though, just to prove him wrong. But what if that was his game? She wasn't ready for this. She didn't want to play games, she didn't want to play at all.

'Let me introduce the show's producer, Gail Cameron. She will run through the details, answer any questions and take care of the legalities. You don't have to make a decision today,' he said as he continued to hold her in his sights, 'but filming starts tomorrow and it would be great if some of you are on board by then.'

He broke eye contact with her as he looked around the table at the other staff members and Annie felt some of the heat leaving her body as he looked away, almost as though a cloud had passed across the sun, casting a shadow over her.

'We're not here to sensationalise things,' he continued. 'We're here to tell stories, to raise awareness and, as I'm sure Patrick has told you, Blue Lake Hospital, and therefore your departments, will benefit financially.'

Annie decided she didn't want anyone accusing her of being difficult or obstructive and she was well aware the hospital could always use extra funds. She'd pretend to give the situation due consideration.

And then she'd say no.

Patrick stood up and moved chairs around, making room for Caspar and Gail to sit at the table. Annie couldn't help but notice that Caspar waited for Gail to sit first and his manners earned him a brownie point, but he still had a long way to go in her opinion.

Annie studied him as he stood beside the table, waiting for Gail to get settled.

He was wearing a single-breasted suit, pale grey in colour, with a plain white shirt and a striped tie. His shoulders were broad and square and filled the suit jacket out very nicely. His shirt was crisply ironed but the suit was a little crumpled. Perhaps, despite being Australia's latest celebrity pin-up, appearances weren't at the top of his list of priorities. Annie decided she could like that about the man, even if she didn't have to like him being here.

He undid the buttons on his jacket and held his tie against his stomach, keeping it out of the way, as he sat in his own chair. His stomach was flat and lean and Caspar was slimmer in real life than he'd appeared on television, but then she remembered that the camera supposedly added pounds. Did, in fact, add pounds. She knew that from her own limited experience.

Gail was speaking, saying something about the types of medical cases they were interested in, and Annie knew she should be listening but her attention kept wandering. Caspar was rolling a pen through his fingers and the movement caught her eye. His fingers were long and slender and his hands were large. Annie could imagine him cradling the newborn babies in his care, holding them nestled safely in the palms of his hands.

Now that he was sitting down, diagonally opposite her, Annie had less of him to peruse. His head was turned to his left, slightly away from her, leaving her looking at his profile. Leaving her free to study him. There were flecks of grey at his temples, a touch of salt and pepper in his black curls, and his olive skin was darkened by the shadow of designer stubble on his jaw. His nose was perfectly straight but maybe a touch longer than it needed to be, which was a good thing, Annie thought, as it stopped him from being too good looking.

Was there such a thing as too good looking? She'd never wondered about that before.

His green eyes were scanning the room, working his way around the table in a clockwise direction as he studied each person present in the meeting, and Annie wondered what he was thinking.

He was looking at Colin, one of the orthopaedic surgeons, and Annie knew it was only a matter of time before his gaze landed on her. She felt her heart rate increase with that thought. For some reason this made her nervous. Her palms felt sweaty and she wiped them on her trousers.

Caspar was watching Tori now but Tori seemed oblivious to his inspection. She had her head down and was furiously taking notes. That was good. She and Tori had formed a close friendship in the six months since she herself had moved to Mount Gambier and she could use Tori's notes to catch up later on everything she hadn't heard Gail say.

And then it was her turn. She'd meant to look away before his gaze reached her but she hadn't and now he was looking straight at her, his green eyes locked with hers. Annie could feel herself begin to blush again under his scrutiny. The heat started over her sternum and she knew it was only a matter of time before it spread to her face, but she was unable to break the connection.

Until Tori nudged her with her elbow.

'Ow,' Annie complained. But it was enough to get her to glance to her right.

'Are you paying attention?' Tori asked. 'You need to listen to this.'

'I'll read your notes later,' Annie told her, but as she turned her head away from Tori she deliberately sought out Gail's face as she pretended to listen and tried to keep Caspar St Claire out of her line of sight. She'd expected his attention to have moved on to the next person at the table but from the corner of her eye she could see that he was still watching her and she couldn't help but move her head, ever so slightly, to look back at him.

He appeared to be concentrating and she wondered again what he was thinking. What he thought about her. His expression seemed to be challenging her but she wasn't sure what his challenge was. Did he want her to question him or back down? If he wanted her to give in on the very first day he was going to be sorely disappointed. She had no intention of giving in, not today and not tomorrow.

She met his gaze as she thought about all the ways she could say no but then his intense expression gave way to a smile and his seriousness dissolved into something else altogether. Something slightly carnal and iniquitous, and Annie forgot all about reality television, all about the cameras invading the hospital, all about saying no as his smile raced through her.

It lit a fire in her belly that poured through her, warming everything from her face to her toes and everything in between, until she felt as though her insides might melt together in a big pool of lust. She'd thought his serious, brooding expression had been handsome but his smile transformed his face completely and now his expression was cheeky and playful and made her think of sex. Something she hadn't thought about for a long time.

Sex wasn't something that had ever been high

on her list of priorities. She enjoyed it but she didn't really see what all the fuss was about. She was quite happy being celibate. But Caspar St Claire made her think of sex. And not the type of sex she was used to. He made her think of hot, sweaty, take-no-prisoners sex. Tangled bedsheets and late-afternoon sex. The weight of a hard, firm, male body. He made her think of multiple orgasms and sex that was so all-consuming she'd be too exhausted to be able to move afterwards. The kind of sex she'd read about in novels and seen in movies but had never experienced.

The temperature in the room felt as though it had increased by several degrees and Annie could feel her nipples harden as her imagination worked overtime. That was enough to make her break eye contact. She looked away hurriedly, almost guiltily, afraid he would be able to see her shameless thoughts.

Her ill-fated marriage had been based on lots of things but desire hadn't been one of them. She'd been a young, inexperienced bride and her marriage had been more about companionship and less about physical attraction or raging hormones. At the time she'd thought she was making a sensible choice. She had seen her parents' relationship self-combust repeatedly and theirs had definitely been a physical thing. As a teenager she'd decided she wouldn't make the same mistake. The trouble was she just made a different one.

But she'd never felt such a strong, unexpected stirring of desire before and to have it triggered by a complete stranger disturbed her. She didn't want to be affected by him. She didn't want to be affected by anybody. As far as she was concerned, that was asking for trouble.

She was going to put Caspar St Claire and everything he was associated with into a mental box marked 'Do not open'. She didn't need to worry about him or his business. It was going to be nothing to do with her.

CHAPTER TWO

CASPAR LOOKED AROUND the table, watching the people, reading their faces, trying to guess their thoughts. Some of them were harder than others. He'd done his research so he knew who they were. He'd found it paid to be prepared—life was challenging enough often enough that he didn't want to deal with unnecessary surprises.

Most looked receptive to Gail's spiel; she made the show sound exciting and new, something people would want to be a part of. Most people. The reality was that it was the editing that would make the show exciting. It was in post-production that the tears and the drama, the heartache, the relief and joy would be enhanced. That was when the emotions would be increased and amplified. For the hospital staff it would really be business as usual. But with cameras.

Gail would make a good salesperson, Caspar

thought as his gaze travelled around the group. He didn't have a clear view of the hospital director, Patrick, as Gail was blocking his line of sight, but that didn't matter. He knew he was on board. Ravi Patel, general surgeon, was sitting beside Patrick. He was watching Gail intently and nodding his head in all the right places. Caspar would bet his precious sports car that Ravi would sign the paperwork before the day was finished.

The RMOs from the emergency department were next. They were shooting glances at Colin Young, one of the hospital's two orthopaedic surgeons. They would take their cues from him and the fact that he was in this meeting led Caspar to believe that he was agreeable to the project. The director of nursing was to Caspar's right. He already knew that Maxine, and therefore her nursing staff, was ready to go. Which left only two—Dr Tori Williams, anaesthetist, and Dr Annie Simpson, obstetrician.

They were seated diagonally opposite him around the oval table. Dr Williams was hunched over the table, furiously taking notes, but he couldn't see her face and he didn't know whether

her note-taking was a positive sign or not. He watched her scribbling for a few more moments but his mind had already moved on to the next person at the table.

Dr Annie Simpson. Patrick Hammond had sent him a short biography of each of the department heads and he recalled what little he'd read about Dr Simpson. Obstetrician, aged twenty-nine, single, trained in Adelaide and started work at Blue Lake Hospital six months ago.

Obviously intelligent and attractive, his mind added a few more adjectives for good measure and he decided he'd have to find out whether 'single' meant unmarried or not in a relationship at all.

If he was honest he'd admit he'd been looking forward to meeting her since he'd seen the photo Patrick had included. He'd specifically asked for photos so he'd be able to identify everyone but he had to admit that Annie's photo hadn't done her justice.

It was a good photo, she was an attractive woman, but it hadn't done justice to the glossy shine of her brown hair or the creaminess of her skin. It hadn't highlighted her sharply defined cheekbones that gave structure to her elfin face neither had it captured her scent.

Standing behind her as he'd entered the room, he'd caught a soft scent of jasmine, which could have come from any one of the women in the space but somehow he'd known it belonged to Annie. The fire in her dark brown eyes had been another surprise. Her eyes had burned with barely contained disapproval, which she hadn't attempted to hide.

He'd expected a lot of things but her passionate objection was something he hadn't anticipated. But he wasn't one to back down from a challenge and he suspected that was just as well.

He'd found it interesting that when Dr Simpson had voiced her concerns no one else had spoken up. Did that mean that she was the only one with concerns or just that she was the only one forthright enough to voice them?

He could see her now in the corner of his eye. A petite woman, she was sitting with perfect posture, her spine stiff and straight, self-control evident. Whatever she might be lacking in size she'd certainly made up for in spirit, but he wondered if she would have been so forthright if she'd known he and Gail could hear every word.

He turned his head to look at her properly. Her shiny curtain of hair fell smoothly down each side of her face, framing it perfectly. Dark chocolate-brown eyes, the colour of which contrasted sharply with her creamy complexion, looked back at him and as he watched he could see two crimson patches of heat appearing over her chiselled cheekbones.

The only other contrasting colour on her face was the soft, plump swell of her pink lips. She held his gaze and he could see the challenge in her brown eyes demanding he convince her of the merits of this project.

Yep, he reckoned, she would have told him straight to his face if she'd known he was standing behind her within earshot. He got the impression she wasn't one to hold back.

Well, challenge accepted, he thought. He needed her on side and he wouldn't rest until she came on board.

Along with the television project he had his own

reasons for coming to Mount Gambier. He'd suggested Blue Lake Hospital as a potential location because it suited him and he wasn't about to sit here and see the project fall apart now. It needed to go ahead and in order to work it really needed the support of the existing hospital staff. And not just one or two of them, he needed them all.

The television network hadn't brought anyone other than him across from the previous series. The budget, with the hospital board's permission, was being used to bolster the hospital coffers, and there wasn't any money to pay extra doctors. The project needed to use the doctors and nurses that were to hand.

He would do whatever it took to convince Dr Simpson of that. He just needed to find out what she wanted. And work out how to give it to her.

He smiled at her, giving her the smile he'd always used on his older sisters when he'd wanted to get his own way, but this time there was no answering smile. No response at all from Dr Simpson, unless he counted the turning of her head to look away. Not the outcome he'd wanted, he had to admit, but there was still time. This had to work.

* * *

Annie couldn't get out of the meeting room fast enough once Gail wrapped up the session. She had no desire to hang around under Caspar's inspection. No desire to be coerced into signing consent forms. And she wasn't prepared for further discussions about why she was so against the idea of appearing on television. Her reasons were none of his business. All he needed to know was that she wasn't interested. In any of it.

She dragged Tori to the staff cafeteria, desperate for a coffee fix after the stress and strain of the meeting. She couldn't think straight while he was watching her with his heavy-eyed green gaze. Her mental picture of him tangled in his sheets was proving hard to shift and even though she knew it was entirely a product of her imagination she was mortified that her mind had taken her there, and she knew she had to put some distance between them if she was going to be able to keep those lustful thoughts out of her head.

She needed some distance if she was going to be able to focus on her job. But if she'd thought she was going to escape discussing the hottest topic in the hospital, she was mistaken.

The cafeteria was buzzing with the news and even Tori, despite bringing Annie to task for staring at Caspar earlier when she should have been listening to Gail, couldn't resist bringing him into their conversation now. 'What have you got against him?' she wanted to know.

'It's not him per se,' Annie tried to explain. 'I just don't want cameras following my every move. I'm here to do a job. I owe it to my patients to give them my best. I don't want people in my way. And that includes him.'

The idea of cameras watching her terrified her. Twice in her life she had been the subject of media attention and neither time had the experience been pleasant, but the thought of working in close proximity to Caspar St Claire, of having him watch her with his bedroom eyes, was even more terrifying. She didn't know if she'd be able to concentrate under his gaze and that made her feel vulnerable. And feeling vulnerable was not something she enjoyed.

'Well, I think he's here to stay,' Tori told her. 'At least for the next eight weeks. And you'll probably be working quite closely with him. He'll be responsible for the care of all those little new-borns you deliver. I don't see how you can avoid him. Or why you'd want to.'

Annie sighed. Tori was right. She was going to have to come up with a solution. She was going to have to work out how to cope with the situation, as unpleasant as it seemed. 'I suppose I can't avoid him,' she agreed, 'but I should be able to avoid being on camera. They'll soon get sick of taking footage of the back of my head and then hopefully they can leave me alone to get on with my job.'

Tori was laughing. 'You're amazing. You'd have to be the only female in the entire hospital who would complain about having to spend time with Dr Tall, Dark and Handsome. Enjoy it. You'll be the envy of all the women in town.'

Annie couldn't imagine being able to enjoy one single minute of it and she'd happily swap places with Tori. With anyone, for that matter. 'I'm sure you'll get your turn, he's bound to need your services while he's here,' she replied. 'You can make sure you have yourself on the roster when they're filming. You can show your face on camera and then they won't need me.'

'I'll be in Theatre with a mask over my face,' Tori grumbled, as she picked up her coffee and moved away from the counter. 'Hey, maybe you could just start wearing a mask for your con-sults—that would solve your problem.'

Annie didn't bother to respond to that com-ment. She just glared at Tori as she stirred milk into her coffee but Tori wasn't finished.

'Caspar St Claire.' She sighed. 'He even sounds like a movie star.'

Annie snorted. 'He probably changed his name for television. I mean, really, who has a name like that?'

'You don't like my name, Dr Simpson?'

Damn it. Annie closed her eyes and groaned si-lently. He'd sneaked up on her and caught her out again. She was going to have to be more careful. She opened her eyes to find Tori trying to stifle a smile. Great. She turned round and came face to face with Dr Tall, Dark and Handsome.

He wasn't trying to stifle a smile. In fact, he was smirking. At her expense. How she'd love to wipe that look off his face but the only way she could think of doing that was by telling him she didn't like his name. And that wasn't true. It was a name that rolled smoothly off the tongue, a name that wouldn't be easily forgotten. Smooth and unforgettable. Much like the man himself, she guessed. Real or not, his name suited him.

'You have a very nice name,' she admitted grudgingly, 'but it's unusual enough to make me wonder if you made it up.' She had to tilt her head back to look up into his face. He was several inches taller than her, an inch or two over six feet, she guessed, and from her viewpoint the strong angles of his jaw, darkened by the shadow of his beard, were even more obvious.

'I admit it's unusual but I assure you it's the name my parents gave me. I can't practise medicine under any other,' he replied.

Annie shrugged. He'd made a fair point.

'I seem to be needing to assure you of a lot of things, Dr Simpson.' He was standing close enough that Annie could see where his day's growth of beard was beginning to darken his jaw and she could feel his breath on her face as he spoke. She looked down, away from his inquisitive green eyes, but she was still aware of the little puffs of soft, warm air that smelt of peppermint and brushed her cheekbones when he spoke to her.

'Is there anything else that's bothering you?' he asked. 'I'd really like you to be on board with this project. As the hospital's obstetrician and paediatrician our paths will cross often, and if we can find a way to work together I think it will be to everyone's advantage. Should we clear the air some more while we have time?'

She looked up again, dragging her eyes away from the broad expanse of his chest to meet his eyes. At this distance she could see they were flecked with brown. Annoyed with herself for noticing, she retorted, 'You may have the time, Dr St Claire, but I'm very busy so if you'll excuse me I have patients to see.'

She knew she sounded snippy but he was standing too close. She was too aware of him. Of his green eyes, of his broad shoulders, of his breath on her skin, and his proximity was playing havoc with her senses, making it impossible for her to think. She couldn't cope with him in her personal space. She hadn't worked out how she was going to deal with him yet. Not in her hospital or in her life. She needed distance. It was the only thing that was going to work for her. She needed to leave. Now.

She picked up her coffee, gripping the cardboard cup so tightly it was in danger of being crushed, and stalked off, glaring at Tori to make sure her friend followed her. She didn't want to leave her consorting with the enemy.

'That was rude,' Tori admonished as she hurried to keep pace with Annie. 'You'll need to play nicely. He could arrange to make you look bad on camera.'

'He wouldn't!' Annie's stride faltered. She hadn't stopped to consider the consequences of her behaviour.

'No, probably not,' Tori admitted. 'If you'd been listening to Gail you would have heard that their intention isn't to paint any of us in a bad light but to give people an insight into what goes on inside a hospital. But I'm sure they're not averse to showing any sparks that might be flying between patients and their families or families and staff or even just between the staff. And where those sparks come from is probably irrelevant—antagonistic or friendly, they all make for good television. But don't forget, Gail's first priority will be to Caspar. She has no loyalty to you so my advice is to play nicely.'

Annie cursed her bad luck. Why had the television network decided to film here? All she wanted was to be left in peace, to be left alone to do her work. Working under the scrutiny of cameras wasn't part of her agenda. She didn't want to be in the spotlight and she had no intention of being a celebrity doctor.

If she didn't give permission to include her in the series then Caspar St Claire wouldn't have the opportunity to make her look bad. But she supposed it wouldn't hurt to play nicely just in case. But it would be even better if she could avoid him altogether.

That plan worked for the rest of the afternoon. Almost.

Annie was heading home, exiting through the main lobby, when the front page of the local paper caught her eye. Caspar was smiling up at her from the centre of the page, looking just as handsome in black and white as he did in the flesh. Curiosity got the better of her and she stopped and picked up the paper, noticing that it was a couple of days old already.

She flicked it open and as she unfolded it Caspar's photographed companion came into view. A tall, attractive blonde woman, Annie recognised her as the host of a popular light entertainment show. Her curiosity piqued further, she began to read the article. Naturally it started by espousing Caspar's talents as the local boy who was returning to his home town as a celebrity doctor and went on to talk about the success of the television series. Annie opened the paper, turning to page four to continue reading, interested to see what the journalist had to say about the woman on Caspar's arm.

'Anything interesting in there?'

Annie jumped as Caspar's warm-treacle tones broke her concentration, interrupting her before she got to the gossip. She looked up, taking in his narrow hips, grey suit and broad shoulders almost as a reflex before her eyes came to rest on his face. One corner of his mouth lifted in the beginning of a smile and she could see the humour in his eyes as he waited for her to deny that she'd been reading about him. But there was no use pretending she hadn't been hunting for information.

'You interrupted me before I got to the good bit,' she replied.

The smile that had been threatening to begin now broke across his face as he laughed. 'If there's anything you need to know, why don't you ask me? I'll trade you a question for a question.'

She tried to ignore the way his smile made his eyes sparkle, triggering the tremble in her stomach. 'Mount Gambier is a long way from the bright lights of Melbourne. How did the network convince you to come here?' she asked.

Annie herself had moved to Mount Gambier happily, hoping the regional location and the job opportunity would give her a chance to rebuild her life, but in her mind the country town seemed a strange choice not only for the television series but also for Caspar St Claire. Regardless of the fact he'd been raised here, she knew he hadn't lived in the Mount for a long time and she wondered what had made him agree to return. With his confident manner and his high profile he seemed far more suited to a big city hospital and to the perks his celebrity status would bring him in a city like Melbourne.

'I wanted to come.'

'Why?' she asked.

'That's two questions,' he said, as he shook his head at her. 'I believe it's my turn now. What are you doing after work?'

His question surprised her. She opened her mouth to say 'Nothing' but quickly realised that, depending on his motives, she might be opening herself up for an unwanted invitation. She closed her mouth, biting back her reply as she tried to think of a different answer.

'Going to the gym,' she told him. That was sort of true. It was what she should be doing, although it wasn't what she felt like and she knew she'd probably skip it altogether, but he didn't need to know that. Just like he didn't need to know her stomach was fluttering with nerves. She told herself it was because she found his presence irritating but she knew she was also bothered because she found him attractive and there was no way she wanted him to know that either.

She wished she could ignore his good looks but she suspected she was going to find that difficult. She'd just have to ignore him instead, she thought as she made a show of checking her watch.

'I'll see you tomorrow, then,' he replied, leaving her wondering why he'd asked in the first place, but his answer served to remind her that it was going to be impossible to ignore him completely. Whether she liked it or not, they would be working together.

Annie hung back as Caspar headed for the exit. She stuck with her pretence of being busy as she didn't want to walk out with him. From the hospital foyer she watched as he climbed into his car. He drove a silver Audi TT, which was definitely a car for a big-city doctor, and she wondered how much the television network was paying him, before reminding herself that he, and therefore his circumstances, was none of her business.

* * *

Annie briefly considered skipping her after-work gym class but she knew Tori would expect a decent reason before she'd allow her to opt out. They'd made a commitment to exercise together, hoping that would make them take it more seriously, and 'Can't be bothered' wasn't going to get her off the hook. She changed into her gym gear at the hospital so she could avoid going home first. She knew that if she went home the temptation to pour a glass of wine and sit on the couch and think about how her day had gone pear-shaped would be too much. In retrospect she decided that going to the gym might help keep her mind off her day.

'So, did you decide to sign the network's consent form?' Tori asked when they met before their gym class.

'Not yet. Have you?'

Tori nodded. 'I'm really excited about the project. Not to mention working with Caspar. Phil is a terrific paediatrician but he's old enough to be my father. I think we've got a pretty good deal having Caspar take over while Phil is on leave.

I can't think of many better ways to spend my theatre time than watching Caspar St Claire.'

Tori had a point but Annie didn't agree whole-heartedly. 'I would have preferred him to be here minus the cameras, though,' she replied. She had been on television before and both occasions had been unpleasant, to say the least. Traumatic would be a better way to describe it. She didn't relish the idea of being exposed to the cameras.

And she knew that was how she was feeling—exposed and vulnerable. Annie had found Tori's support and friendship invaluable since she'd moved to the Mount but Tori still only knew half the story as far as Annie's history went. She thought about telling Tori the whole truth but now wasn't the time or the place.

'Unfortunately it doesn't work that way,' Tori said. 'The cameras are part of the package. Look at it this way—you want your contract renewed, don't you? I think taking part in this series would be a very good way of getting support for an extension of your contract.'

The instructor called them all to order and the class began putting an end to their conversation.

Annie wasn't fit enough to talk and exercise at the same time but she was co-ordinated enough to be able to exercise and think about Tori's comment.

Her contract with the hospital was for twelve months. She needed it to be extended. She needed the job and needed the money. As much as she hated the idea of being on television, she knew Tori was right. She didn't have a choice. She couldn't afford to be choosy or create waves. She would have to sign the agreement and she would have to work with Caspar St Claire.

Avoiding Caspar for one afternoon had been a good start but she couldn't avoid him for ever and, in case she'd forgotten the fact, she had an early reminder when she arrived at the hospital the following morning. Parked almost outside the front doors was a large van emblazoned with the television network logo.

Filming was due to start today and it appeared they were ready and raring to go. Just thinking about it made her insides tremble. She actually felt nauseous at the thought of the camera crew dogging her steps.

Annie sighed as she made her way into the hospital and upstairs to the maternity ward. She had little doubt her path would cross with Caspar's at some point today.

She still hadn't signed the agreement, but she planned to do it later that day. She was hoping to delay it just a little longer to buy herself one more day, one more day when she would be safe from observation.

She kept her head down as she hurried past the nursery, too afraid to look through the large glass door in case she saw him—she was keen to avoid an inevitable meeting for as long as possible. She stopped briefly at the nurses' station to check for any updates before rushing to begin her rounds, rushing to hide behind the sanctuary of ward room curtains and doors.

Once she was among her patients she slowed her pace, ambling through her rounds. She wasn't consulting until the afternoon so she took her time, hoping that Caspar would be long gone from the floor before she emerged again. When she eventually finished she returned to the nurses' station to sign case notes but she made sure she kept her back to the wall, not wanting to give Caspar another opportunity to sneak up on her and overhear any conversations. She had no idea where he was but she wasn't taking any chances.

However, within a few minutes she realised he must be on the floor. Nurses started appearing from all corners of the wing, from patients' bedsides, the tearoom and even the pan room, as if there had been a silent announcement about events unfolding. And the only thing Annie could think of that would have the nurses all heading into the corridors would be if word had got around that Caspar St Claire was coming their way.

She glanced up from the notes and wasn't surprised to see him walking towards the desk with nurses trailing in his wake, almost falling over themselves as they rushed to offer their help. One of the nurses, whose name Annie thought was Tiffany, almost knocked down another in her desperate hurry to get to Caspar first.

The scene was rather amusing and Annie found she was smiling to herself and feeling positive for the first time since Caspar had arrived at Blue Lake Hospital. But that didn't mean she wanted to deal with him this morning. She thought about pretending she hadn't seen him and making her escape, running away and hiding again. But it was too late. He was heading her way. And smiling. At her.

Did he think her smile was for him? She supposed he would. He had no reason to think she was smiling to herself about the unfolding tableau.

She had to admit he had a really lovely smile. A crease appeared on either side of his mouth, running down to his jaw. They framed his lips and accentuated his square jaw, and the brooding expression in his eyes was replaced with laughter. It was all too easy to keep smiling back at him in return but she needed to remember that she wasn't one of the young, impressionable nurses and she had to remember that he wasn't Dr Tall, Dark and Handsome to her. He was Dr Disturbing-her-peaceful-life.

Annie wiped the smile from her face as he drew nearer but she hadn't completely forgotten Tori's warning to play nicely.

'Good morning,' she greeted him. 'Are you finding your way around all right?'

'Yes. Everyone's being very helpful,' he replied, but he looked at her for a moment longer than he needed to and Annie could almost hear the unspoken words. *Except for you.*

Well, that was too bad for him. She imagined he was used to getting his own way but that didn't mean he deserved to. And if Tiffany and the other nurses on this ward were the yardsticks then she didn't doubt the females on staff were being extremely helpful.

'Where is the crew?' she asked, choosing to ignore his unspoken implication.

'They're busy doing their own checks. They need to do some run-throughs before we start— lighting, sound, that sort of thing.'

She'd expected to see him with an entourage. 'How many of them are there?'

'Only a few,' he answered. 'Liam, the cameraman, Keegan for sound and lighting, and you met Gail, the producer.'

'No make-up?'

'No make-up.'

That would explain why he looked so good in the flesh. Dr Tall, Dark and Handsome wasn't made up for the cameras. The thought didn't make her feel any better. She still wasn't sure how she felt about men who were so good looking.

She'd thought his nose was slightly too long but standing directly in front of him now even that looked perfect and she knew she'd just been searching for flaws. It was hard to fault him physically.

'Apparently our production budget is very modest, which is why the network can afford to be generous towards the hospital. We don't have a lot of expenses.'

'What about your fee? They must pay you?' She remembered his sleek silver sports car and the words were out of her mouth before she realised how rude she sounded. 'Sorry, ignore that, it's none of my business.' She was desperate to change the subject and she looked around quickly, searching for another topic of conversation.

The nurses, having all come out of the wood-work, were now milling around, pretending to look busy, but Annie could see they were all there to check Caspar out. She remembered how he'd known everyone in the meeting yesterday and wondered if his extensive knowledge included the nurses.

'Do I need to introduce you or have you mem-orised everyone's names?' she asked as she ges-tured towards the nurses.

'I didn't have time to learn everybody's name, just the most important ones,' he replied as he zeroed in on her with his green eyes. He was watching her intently and she felt as though he was putting her under the microscope.

'So what was that little party trick all about?' Annie was vaguely aware of the ward phone ring-ing as she tried to concentrate under the force of Caspar's gaze.

'Which one?'

'That stunt yesterday, knowing who we were?'

'It wasn't a stunt. I figured I was going to be

at a disadvantage. You know each other already but I'm going to be working with you all and the quicker I get everyone straight in my head the faster I'll settle in. I like to be prepared.'

'Dr Simpson?' Ellen, one of the more experienced midwives, interrupted them. She had answered the phone and she covered the mouthpiece with her hand as she spoke to Annie. 'I have one of your patients on the phone, Kylie Jones. She says her waters have broken. Do you need me to pull up her file?'

Annie shook her head. 'No, that's all right.' She knew Kylie. 'Is her husband home?'

'I'll check,' Ellen replied, but within a few seconds she was shaking her head. 'He's not due back until next week.'

Annie knew that Paul Jones worked in mining, which meant he worked away for two weeks before coming home for two. 'Tell her we'll send an ambulance for her. She needs to be in here. If she's up to it she can contact Paul while she's waiting so he can organise to get home as soon as possible.'

Annie turned to Caspar. She couldn't believe she was about to ask this of him.

'Kylie is thirty-three weeks pregnant with twins. I'm going to need your help.'

'Of course.' He grinned at her and the sparkle returned to his eyes. Annie felt that funny warmth rush through her, as though his smile was the match and her belly was full of dry tinder. 'I thought you'd never ask,' he said as he pulled his phone from his pocket.

'What are you doing?'

'Calling the camera crew.'

'What? No!' she protested.

'What do you mean, "no"? This is what we're here for.'

Annie disagreed. 'Why do you want to film Kylie? What's the point? You have no back story, no history with her.' *And I don't want a camera crew in my delivery suite.*

But Caspar wasn't going to back down easily.

'We can do all that afterwards,' he said, unperturbed. 'We can follow her story and follow the babies' progress.'

Somehow she'd known he wouldn't give in.

'These babies are premature,' she argued. 'They have to survive first.'

As she debated the situation she realised that from the television perspective it probably didn't matter if the babies survived or not. Either way it would be high drama. But to his credit Caspar didn't point that depressing fact out to her. In fact, he seemed to try to make an effort to reassure her.

'I am a paediatrician, this is what I do. You have to trust me, I am very good at my job and just like you I swore an oath to do no harm.' His brooding expression was back, his green eyes darker now, his jaw set. 'This is a perfect story for the show—a premature delivery of twins with the father not able to make it for the birth. It's in my best interests to make sure it has a happy ending and then we'll be able to film an emotional reunion scene as well.'

'You're forgetting something,' Annie argued. 'I'll be in the delivery suite and I haven't given my permission to be filmed.'

Caspar shrugged. 'We'll keep you out of the shot. It's Kylie and the babies we want. We can

use voiceovers, music, whatever we need to elim-
inate anything you say as well if you prefer. The
wonders of modern technology.'

'Are you telling me you'll film without my permission?'

'Are you always this argumentative?' he asked
as a broad grin broke across his face and his eyes
sparkled again.

*Was he smiling at her? Did he find her amus-
ing? Did he think she didn't mean business?*

She didn't know where to look as she tried to
ignore the funny tumbling sensation in her stomach. All she knew was that he was responsible
for the feeling and that frightened her. She didn't
want to be attracted to him. She couldn't imagine dealing with that on top of working with him.
The stress made her belligerent. 'Only when I
think people are wrong,' she snapped.

'But I'm not wrong. We can edit you out but
you can't stop us from filming. I have the hospital's permission and all I need is Kylie's. If you
like, I promise to show you the edited version
before it goes to air.'

By God, the man was irritating. 'I have no idea

whether I can trust you to keep your promises, though, do I?' Annie had learned through bitter experience that some people lied, cheated, made promises they had no intention of keeping and let others down on a regular basis. And to trust someone she barely knew didn't sit comfortably with her.

'This discussion could well be moot anyway,' Caspar said. 'It all depends on Kylie now.'

He pressed a button on his phone and made the call while Annie stood by, fuming silently. If he thought he could win every time by being stubborn she had news for him, but she knew that his chances of getting his own way were better than hers. Kylie's babies would need Caspar St Claire. Annie couldn't do this without him.

She could hope that Kylie would choose not to invite the cameras into the delivery suite but if that didn't happen Annie knew she'd have to relent. She hated feeling powerless. She had sworn an oath to herself to take charge of her life, not to let other people dictate things to her, but ever since Caspar had walked into the hospital she could feel control being wrested from her.

She'd thought she would be able to avoid him and his cameras but she realised now that it wasn't going to be her decision and, what was even worse, she realised that there would be times when she'd need him and she'd have to acquiesce.

'Now, why don't we agree to put our differences aside and you can tell me about Kylie,' Caspar said as he ended his phone call. 'Regardless of whether or not we film this delivery, I will be taking care of the babies, so is there anything I need to know? Has she had any medical complications? Have there been any issues with the pregnancy?'

Before Annie could answer any of his questions they were interrupted by Ellen. 'The ambulance is nearly here.'

'I want to meet the paramedics,' Annie told him as she resigned herself to the fact that she was going to have to work with him. 'If you come with me I'll fill you in on the way, but her pregnancy has been pretty straightforward. She's young, twenty-three, first pregnancy, fraternal twins. I'm not expecting any problems aside from the usual premmie issues.'

They arrived at the ambulance bay as the paramedics were opening the ambulance doors. Caspar was on the phone again and Annie could hear him instructing the crew to meet them in Emergency. She hoped Caspar was able to focus on more than one thing at a time. He needed to. Time would tell.

'You know this patient?' the paramedic checked as Annie introduced herself, and when she nodded, he continued. 'Her waters have broken for at least one twin. Her blood pressure is elevated, one-sixty-five over ninety-five, and foetal heart rates are both around one-forty.'

'Any contractions?'

'A couple of mild ones. Several minutes apart.'

Annie spoke to one of the nurses who had followed them out to the ambulance. 'Can you page Dr Williams and get her down here?' she asked. Kylie's blood pressure was much higher than she'd like and an epidural might help, but she'd let Tori decide.

The paramedics retrieved the stretcher with her

patient and Annie bent over her, talking quietly. 'Kylie, welcome. I wasn't expecting you quite so soon. We're going to take you into the emergency department and see what your babies are up to.' Annie needed to determine how far along Kylie was. She didn't need her wanting to push as they were on their way to Maternity.

She was aware of Caspar hovering at her right shoulder. She had to introduce him to Kylie as, like it or not, he was going to be part of this. But he wasn't waiting for her. He stepped around her and spoke to Kylie.

'Hello, Kylie, I'm—'

'Caspar St Claire,' Kylie gasped. 'I've seen you on telly. What are you doing here?'

Of course, Annie thought, Caspar's fame would have preceded him. Annie wasn't quite sure how Kylie had found the energy to gush over Caspar. Surely if she was in labour she should have more pressing things to think about.

'We're filming the next series of *RPE* here at Blue Lake Hospital. Would you like to be a part of it?' Caspar asked as Kylie was wheeled through the hospital doors.

'You'll deliver my babies? On telly?'

Annie felt her temper rising but Caspar shook his head and quickly put Kylie straight.

'No, Dr Simpson will deliver your babies but I'll be right here, ready to look after them as soon as they are born. We'll get it all on camera and you'll have a perfect recording of the whole experience to show your husband when he gets back to town.'

And with those words Annie knew Caspar would win the argument. Kylie was already looking at him as if he could give her the moon—knowing that her husband was going to miss the birth of their babies had to be bothering her. If Caspar could solve that problem by taping the birth, not only for national television but for Kylie's husband, then there was no way Kylie would kick him out of the delivery suite.

'I'll feel better if you are here, Dr St Claire.' Kylie turned her head to look at Annie. 'Can you imagine, Dr Simpson? My family on national telly.'

And just like that Annie found herself overruled. She knew she had to be a gracious loser and she didn't have time to argue anyway. Her patient was her first priority, her only priority, and she had more pressing concerns—Kylie's blood pressure for one—than whether or not her patient wanted her fifteen minutes of fame.

Annie forced herself to smile as she said, 'Okay, then, let's get you inside.'

CHAPTER THREE

THE CAMERA CREW arrived as Kylie was being shifted across onto a hospital bed. Caspar spoke to them quickly as they began to pull equipment from an assortment of bags and trolleys. Annie was relieved to see that there were only two men, as Caspar had told her, but she had no time to pay them any attention as she started to pull the curtains around the cubicle to give Kylie some privacy as they got her changed into a hospital gown.

'Can you give us a minute?' she asked Caspar as she closed the curtains, barely waiting for his nod in reply before she shut him and his crew out. Albeit temporarily. They'd barely got Kylie sorted before Caspar was back in the cubicle. He didn't ask for permission, he simply got on with the job of attaching the foetal heart monitors to Kylie's abdomen.

Annie was about to tell him she could manage but she bit back her sharp retort when she realised that if Phil had been the paediatrician in the cubicle instead of Caspar, she would have been grateful for his assistance. It wasn't Caspar's fault she didn't know how to handle him. She was going to have to find a way though. For her patient's sake.

People were bustling around Kylie and Annie shifted her attention away from Caspar's long fingers, as he stuck electrodes onto their patient, and over to the monitor, which was now displaying Kylie's BP. It had dropped since the paramedic's report. It was now one-fifty over ninety. Still high but not dangerously so. Had Kylie just been apprehensive?

Annie knew that was possible. Going into early labour when your husband was thousands of miles away would be nerve-racking for most people, and looking at her patient now she certainly appeared more relaxed than when she'd arrived. Kylie was lying calmly, staring at Caspar as he finished attaching the electrodes and hooked her up to another monitor.

Maybe Kylie's improved blood pressure had less to do with apprehension and more to do with the visiting specialist, Annie thought, and she just managed to stop herself from rolling her eyes. It seemed Caspar St Claire had this effect on all women, herself included, she admitted grudgingly, but if he was aware of the scrutiny he didn't show any sign of discomfort.

The monitor was displaying two distinct foetal heartbeats. Caspar turned to Annie and gave her a thumbs-up accompanied by a big smile. He was the epitome of someone who was completely in control. He was composed and relaxed and Annie knew his demeanour would help Kylie.

It was time for Annie to take a leaf out of his book and get to work. She straightened her back as she finished drying her hands. She could do cool, calm and collected just as well as he could.

'All right, Kylie,' she said, as she took up her position at the foot of the bed. 'I'll need to do an internal exam to see what's happening. Are you okay with that?'

Annie wondered if she'd need to tell the camera crew what was appropriate for them to film but at the moment they were concentrating on Kylie's face and no doubt were including shots of Caspar's handsome face too, just for good measure. Probably just as well. She supposed they knew what the viewers wanted to see and she'd bet they'd be happier looking at Caspar St Claire than anything she might be able to offer them.

Annie was surprised to find that, despite not reporting much discomfort, Kylie was already several centimetres dilated. She could see Kylie's abdominal muscles ripple as a contraction ran through her. She checked that the nurse had recorded the time as she asked, 'Have you been having contractions for a while?'

'No. They only started after I called the hospital,' Kylie answered.

'Any other aches and pains?'

'My back's been a bit sore today but I spent the past couple of days cleaning the house so I think I just overdid it.'

'Well, it seems that twin one is determined to arrive today. He's in a good position and I'd say you're well into the first stage of labour.'

'Are you telling me I'm too late?'

Annie turned as Tori came into the room. 'I actually wanted your opinion on giving Kylie an epidural to bring her blood pressure down, not for pain relief as such.'

Tori's eyes flicked to the monitor, which showed one-forty over eighty-five. 'Her BP looks okay.'

Annie nodded in agreement. 'It's lowered considerably since she arrived. Kylie is thirty-three weeks, in established labour with twins and coping well with discomfort.'

'I'll hang around for a bit if it's a multiple birth, just in case,' Tori said. 'I assume you've got a theatre on standby?'

Annie nodded. She had a theatre reserved but she hoped she wouldn't need it. She also hoped to avoid delivering the twins in the emergency department. She spoke to Caspar. 'Where would you like me to deliver the twins—here or in a delivery suite in Maternity?'

'I think the environment in Maternity is far more conducive to a relaxed birth,' Caspar replied. 'And it's closer to the paediatric unit and the nursery. That gets my vote.'

'It is much nicer in Maternity,' Annie said to

Kylie. 'More space, windows, music. So if you're okay with it I'll just give you an injection that will help the babies' lungs and then we'll get this show on the road.' She drew up a syringe of corticosteroids and injected it into Kylie before instructing the medical team, 'All right, people, let's get ready to move.'

It took less than ten minutes to get Kylie to Maternity but her labour had progressed rapidly and by the time they reached the delivery suite she was ready to push.

Annie managed to position herself so that Liam and his camera were behind her. That served a dual purpose—she could pretend he wasn't there and the camera could only get pictures of the back of her head. But as she coached Kylie through the birth of the first baby she realised that Liam wasn't interested in her anyway. Just as he'd done in Emergency, he concentrated on Kylie and Caspar.

Even though Annie had talked about the first twin in a masculine form, something she had a habit of doing unless she knew the sex, the first baby was a girl. She was small, with the familiar premmie appearance of too much skin and not enough padding, but perfectly proportioned with the right number of fingers and toes.

Caspar was standing by Annie's shoulder as she delivered the baby. She couldn't see him but she knew he was there. She could feel him. She turned slightly to give him the baby. He was ready and waiting, his hands reaching for the tiny newborn.

As he lifted the baby from Annie's palms, the backs of his hands slid against her skin and Annie had the strangest sensation of heat exploding inside her. She'd noticed his smile had the ability to make her feel as though she was melting but his touch made her feel like she was combusting. How was that possible? Thank goodness she was already sitting down. She knew her legs wouldn't have been able to support her. It felt as though her bones had turned to jelly, as though her limbs were liquid.

And then, as suddenly as she'd been aware of the heat, it was replaced by cold, empty air as he took the baby from her hands.

Annie followed his movements with her eyes.

The tiny baby appeared even more diminutive cradled in his large hands. She swallowed and rubbed her hands together, encouraging the warmth back into them, but she couldn't reproduce that intense heat and now she wondered if she'd just imagined it.

To have her body react on such a level, seemingly uncontrolled by her brain, was a strange concept. She wasn't completely inexperienced, she was a twenty-nine-year-old divorcee, but she'd never felt this sort of visceral, impulsive attraction before. Were other people constantly aware of these feelings? Maybe she was the odd one out.

Surely this sensation must be an extraordinary one because how anyone could get anything done if they were trying to focus while dealing with these feelings was a mystery to her. She needed to get a grip. She couldn't let herself be distracted by Caspar St Claire.

She returned her attention to her patient, annoyed with herself for losing focus. She waited to hear the baby's first cry before she clamped and cut the umbilical cord and began to check the progress of twin number two.

Caspar finished his one-minute Apgar check, pronounced a birth weight of two thousand five hundred grams and handed the baby to a tearful but happy Kylie. Ellen, the midwife, loosened Kylie's gown so she could expose her shoulder and have some skin-to-skin contact with her baby. With the new mum comfortably occupied with her newborn daughter, Caspar's focus returned to Annie. She could sense his attention.

'The amniotic sac is still intact,' Annie told him. The second twin wasn't in such a hurry to be born. 'But the baby is breech.'

'Can you turn it?' he asked, even as Annie was positioning herself to try.

'I think so.' She hoped she could manage. She didn't want Kylie to go through a Caesarean section, not after delivering the first twin so successfully. Managing premature twins was going to be enough for Kylie to deal with without having to recover from major surgery as well.

Annie was relieved when she was able to turn the baby without much difficulty. She checked the monitors, pleased to see that Kylie's blood pressure was within normal limits and so were the unborn twin's vital signs. He wasn't distressed. Annie couldn't stop Kylie's labour now but they could afford to wait for this delivery to happen at its own pace. She sat back and relaxed.

'Good job.'

Caspar's words, delivered in his rich, deep voice, sent a warm glow through her. She glanced up to find he was smiling at her. She smiled back and was aware of that slow burning heat in her stomach again but it was nothing like the roaring fire she'd felt when he'd touched her. The slow burn she could handle but she wasn't so sure how to deal with the rest of it.

She was pleased he was there with her and that was unexpected. They worked well together and she allowed herself to feel an affinity with him. It was good to know they would be able to manage professionally.

'Once Kylie's contractions pick up again I'll do an amniotomy and hopefully we can have another smooth, intervention-free delivery,' she said.

It didn't take long for Kylie's contractions to

build up. By the time Caspar had done his second lot of Apgar scores on the little girl and given her some more bonding time with her mum before placing her into the humidicrib to keep her warm, Kylie's contractions were strong and frequent.

As Annie ruptured the membranes she made a mental note to remind Kylie that she'd have to get to the hospital quickly with her next pregnancy because once she went into labour things happened rapidly.

Annie delivered the baby's anterior shoulder and in between contractions administered an injection of oxytocin into Kylie's thigh before completing the delivery. At two thousand six hundred grams the baby boy was slightly heavier than his older sister.

Caspar waited for Annie to pass the baby to him and even though Annie was prepared for the contact this time, the sensation still made her catch her breath. She concentrated on delivering the placenta while Caspar took care of the second baby. Once he was out of her space it was business as usual. Everyone had a job to do and Annie's focus was on Kylie, yet she was still aware of Caspar.

Annie was inserting a drip into Kylie's arm when the twins were taken off to the nursery. The little boy needed additional oxygen but otherwise Caspar pronounced them healthy. Annie had completely forgotten about Liam and his camera until she noticed him trailing behind Caspar as they headed for the nursery. She couldn't believe she'd been so immersed in the delivery that she had been able to forget they were being filmed.

Ellen had taken Kylie into the en suite bathroom and Annie's job was finished. Caspar and the twins were gone and in a minute Ellen would take Kylie to the nursery as well. Normally Annie would call in at the nursery too if she wasn't needed elsewhere, but she was reluctant to do that today as she didn't want to follow Caspar or the camera. She was due in her office shortly to start her outpatient clinic but she didn't feel like rushing off. She actually felt at a bit of a loose end.

The spark of attraction she felt for Caspar had opened up old wounds. She couldn't deny he was a good-looking man and she knew it was simple chemistry that had her feeling as though she was on fire. But the trouble was, she knew it wasn't simple. In her experience, chemistry rarely was.

She'd seen how complicated things could become when chemistry was part of the equation. She'd seen it with her own parents and she always swore she would never succumb to it. She wanted so badly to be different from her mother. She might find Caspar attractive but she wasn't going to do anything about it. Unlike her mother, she could, and would, resist temptation.

For years she'd listened to her mother talk about how she'd fallen in love with her father at first sight. They hadn't been able to get enough of each other physically, even though they'd been a disaster emotionally. Their tempestuous relationships had come at the expense of all other relationship in their lives, their daughter's most of all.

Her parents spent more time apart than together but when they reunited, initially at least, they had no awareness of anything around them, including their daughter. Nothing existed beyond the two of them. Inevitably, though, when they had satisfied their physical desire to the point where they were able to notice their surroundings again, they began to irritate each other.

Beyond their chemistry they had nothing in common and Annie had promised herself that when she was old enough she wouldn't get caught up in such a physical relationship. She would make sure she chose someone with whom she had could share something beyond the physical. At the age of twenty-one that was exactly what she had done and yet, by the age of twenty-nine, she found herself divorced, childless and homeless.

Since her divorce, delivering other people's babies had always been a bittersweet experience. She loved the whole new-life thing but currently it just reminded her that she was not only divorced she was also not a mother, and as her thirtieth birthday approached she couldn't imagine her situation changing. Along with her house, her marriage and her job, her divorce might have also cost her the chance of having her own family.

But sitting in the delivery suite feeling sorry for herself wasn't achieving anything. She had work to do.

* * *

Caspar had no time to reflect on his first official day at Blue Lake Hospital until he was in his car on the way to dinner. As usual he was running late. He'd organised for the camera crew to film Kylie and her babies in the nursery and of course it had taken longer than planned. But overall the day had been a success. Along with Kylie's story there had been another good case requiring the services of Colin Young, the orthopaedic surgeon. Caspar hadn't been involved in that story but the crew was pleased with the footage they'd taken so they were off to an encouraging start.

But in his mind the biggest success had been getting Annie Simpson to agree to allow filming during the delivery. He had kept his promise and instructed the crew not to focus on her. After all, it was Kylie's story they were telling, but as a paediatrician he knew he would more than likely be spending a large chunk of his time working with Annie, and if they could come to a compatible arrangement that would be ideal.

He'd been impressed with her skills and her unflappable nature. Once again she hadn't held back when it came time to expressing her opinion but he decided that he liked that about her. She wasn't tiptoeing around him or the television network. Her patients came first, as they should, and when they were in her delivery suites she made sure everyone knew she was in charge.

But something told him she'd look great on camera and he was still keen for her agree to that. But for now he was happy just to have her permission to film her with her patients.

As he pulled to a stop at the traffic light outside the Royal Hotel he couldn't resist looking inside and he knew he was looking for Annie. Sitting in the car, he fancied he could still smell her. The sweet, subtle hint of jasmine had stayed with him even though he'd showered and changed, and the scent had him searching for her.

Tiffany, one of the many very friendly and helpful nurses, had invited him to join in for Friday drinks at the hotel but he was already committed to, and now late for, dinner at his sister's. But what if Annie was in there? What if Annie had invited him? Would he have delayed his plans? She was an attractive woman, that hadn't escaped his attention, but she was also intriguing. But no matter how alluring he found her, he couldn't let his sister down. He knew he hadn't been pulling his weight as far as family responsibilities went and he was in Mount Gambier now to share the load. That was why he'd pushed for *RPE* to be filmed here. It suited him.

The light turned green and he drove on down the road, choosing to behave responsibly and resist temptation.

He pulled his car into his sister's driveway, scattering his teenage niece and nephew, who were taking shots at the basketball ring over the garage door.

'You're late,' his niece chastised him as he hugged her.

'Occupational hazard, I'm afraid,' he replied.

'Enough talk. Let's get inside and eat,' his nephew said as he had one last shot at the ring before ushering them along the front path.

'How's Grandpa doing?' Caspar asked as they headed into the house.

'He knows who we are today so that's pretty good,' they told him.

His dad unfolded his lanky frame from the lounge and stood up as Caspar came into the room. He was a tall man and was perhaps a little more stooped than when Caspar had last seen him a few months ago, but other than that he was unchanged.

The old man in front of him was the reason Caspar had pushed for *RPE* to be filmed in Mount Gambier. Basing this series at Blue Lake Hospital had brought him back to his family and would give him time to help sort through the issues involving his father. Dementia was a difficult illness to manage, not least for the families of the sufferers, and Caspar's sisters had been coping for quite a while without any help from him.

Until a couple of weeks ago Joseph St Claire had been staying with his middle child, Kristin, but she had her hands full with two children and a third one due very soon, on top of which she worked with her husband in their winery and lived half an hour from town. Caring for her father as well had become too much to deal with and Joe had moved in with Brigitte.

Joe's grey eyes lit up when he saw Caspar walk through the door. 'Caspar, my boy, how are you?'

Caspar hadn't stopped to consider how he would feel if his father didn't recognise him. He supposed it was ultimately inevitable but he was glad he didn't have to confront that fact today. However, his relief was short-lived.

'How were your final exams?' his father asked.

He'd done his final exams five years ago at the age of twenty-eight.

Brigitte, older than Caspar by eight years, heard the exchange as she came out of the kitchen. 'Hi, baby brother,' she said, as she hugged him, before she expertly changed the subject by announcing, loud enough for everyone else to hear, 'Let's eat.'

'We'll talk later,' she whispered to Caspar, as her family assembled in the dining room.

'Aren't we waiting for your mother?' Joe asked as Brigitte's husband began to carve the roast.

'She's not here tonight, Dad. Do you remember what I told you?'

Caspar watched as his father frowned, obviously concentrating and trying to recall what Brigitte had said to him.

'It's her bridge night,' Brigitte said.

Now it was Caspar's turn to frown. Their mother had died three years ago. What was Brigitte doing?

'I'll explain later.' Brigitte mouthed the words silently across the table.

Caspar attempted to put the exchange to the back of his mind while he tried to enjoy his dinner. Brigitte was a good cook and he couldn't remember the last time he'd had a roast dinner with all the trimmings, but the dramatic decline in his father's condition since he'd last seen him a few months ago concerned him greatly and took the pleasure out of the meal.

He knew it was tinged by guilt. Guilt that he hadn't visited as often as he should and guilt that he'd left his sisters with the burden of caring for their father.

At the end of the meal Brigitte's children helped settle their grandfather for the night while Caspar helped Brigitte in the kitchen. Their father had asked no more questions about their mother's whereabouts during the remainder of the meal and Caspar figured he'd either forgotten she was out, forgotten he'd asked the question or had re-membered she'd died. Caspar didn't know which one of those was right but he was relieved not to have to deal with more questions.

He'd never thought he'd back away from a chal-lenge but this situation was not something he'd had any experience with and he didn't know how to deal with it. Their mother had died from a stroke. Her death had been sudden and trau-matic for all of them but at least they hadn't had to watch as she'd slowly declined. Caspar had no experience with treating the elderly and no experience with treating dementia yet he felt as though he should have something to contribute. He felt as though he was letting his family down.

'Dad's forgotten that Mum died?' he asked Bri-gitte as he scraped plates before stacking them into the dishwasher.

'Sometimes he remembers and sometimes he doesn't. It's too difficult to go through it with him every time. Can you imagine what it would be like to hear for the first time that Mum has died and to have to hear that every few days? It's dis-tressing for him and for us. It's better to say she's out and usually he forgets to ask when she'll be back or he goes to bed and forgets. Tomorrow he might remember again that she's dead and if he does that's okay, but it's better if it's something he can recall rather than reliving the grief over and over again.'

'I didn't realise he'd gone downhill quite so fast.'

'I think moving here from Kristin's has unsettled him a bit,' Brigitte said as she filled the sink with water for the pots and pans. 'But it really hasn't been that quick a decline, Caspar, it's just that you haven't seen him for months.'

There was no criticism in his elder sister's tone, she was just stating facts, but it all added to his guilt. He didn't really have a good excuse. Mount Gambier was only a few hours' drive from his home in Melbourne. His work and filming the last series of *RPE* had kept him busy but filming had wrapped up several months ago and both his sisters worked too yet they had managed to care for their father.

'Tell me what you've been up to. Have you got any juicy bits of celebrity gossip? Are you dating anyone? Is there a story behind that photo I saw of you with the host from that talent show that was on the front page of the paper?'

It seemed Brigitte had developed quite a knack for changing the subject. Caspar went with the new topic. He knew he'd find out soon enough exactly how his father was faring.

'We went out a couple of times but we had nothing in common,' he replied. They'd been quite compatible in the bedroom but his sister didn't need to hear about that, and they'd had absolutely nothing to talk about.

Brigitte laughed. 'Other than both being in reality television shows.'

'Other than that.' Caspar grinned. 'But you know I don't think of myself as a celebrity and I don't really want to date one either.'

'No, you're far too high-brow,' his sister teased.

Despite being on television, he wasn't interested in the television business, but that wasn't because he thought it was beneath him, it was because his focus lay elsewhere.

His interest lay solely with doing as good a job as he could with the show from a medical perspective. He wasn't really interested in the politics of show business, of being seen at the right parties and with the right people. He wasn't planning on having a career in the media. He had a career he loved already, a career that was vastly different from the entertainment business.

He had agreed to be on *RPE* because he wanted to raise awareness of medical conditions and he'd hoped to raise funds for particular causes, but he hadn't really counted on becoming a celebrity himself, however minor.

'No, I just don't want to have a high-profile relationship that's played out in front of the media. I didn't think this series would be as big a success as it is and I would prefer to be able to have a private life that is actually private.'

'You never know, you might be able to date quietly here. No one ever pays any attention to what's happening in the country. Maybe Kristin and I can find you a nice country girl and then you'd have a reason to stay in town. I know exactly the type you need.'

Caspar knew he shouldn't ask but he was intrigued. 'And what type of woman do I need?'

'One with a bit of substance. One who won't always let you get your own way or rule the roost.'

'You make me sound like a bully,' he protested.

'Not at all, but you've always done things on your terms. You like to be in control. You need a girl with enough attitude to stand up to you. One who can hold her own in an argument.'

His thoughts went immediately to a petite brunette with a ballerina's physique and exquisite cheekbones who certainly didn't hold back her opinions. One who was happy to tell him exactly what she thought of him and his ideas. He wondered what his sisters would make of Annie.

He almost laughed out loud at the idea of asking Annie on a date. He could just imagine what she'd say to that.

And what would she make of being splashed across the front of the local paper or in the magazine social pages? He knew she'd be less than impressed. He imagined her aversion to cameras would extend to all types of media and there would be nowhere to hide in a town the size of Mount Gambier, despite what Brigitte thought, and he knew anyone he dated would be of interest to the media.

It was a ridiculous idea. Why was he even thinking about it?

He didn't have time to date. He had other priorities at present. 'Between work and this television show I haven't had time to help you with Dad, so where would I find the time for dating? The PR team for the television show found my last half-dozen dates for me when I needed one.'

That had suited him as it had meant good publicity for the show without requiring too much input from him.

'Well, maybe we could do a better job than the PR department,' Brigitte replied.

'Thanks, but I really don't have time.'

He wasn't interested in a serious relationship. He told himself it was because he didn't have time but he knew that his reluctance stemmed mainly from a belief that happy endings were few and far between. He didn't want to start searching for the perfect woman; he was convinced she didn't exist, and he didn't want to waste time or energy looking for someone who didn't exist. He didn't want the disappointment.

He'd learnt the hard way that he couldn't control other people's actions so he concentrated on what he could control—his own actions. There was never any shortage of eager women to keep him company when he wanted it so there was no reason to look for anything more. Short, casual relationships meant he could retain control and that suited him perfectly.

He didn't believe in fairy-tales. If fairy-tales came true, he wouldn't have been abandoned as a baby. His story had had a happy ending but that had been thanks to the two people who had rescued him and given him a family. Love had a big part to play but he didn't think he could be that lucky a second time. Getting two fairy-tale endings in one lifetime just didn't happen. He didn't want a serious relationship. He didn't need it. He wanted to stay in control.

'And despite what you think,' he added, 'I know that anyone I dated would be fodder for the media, even in the Mount.'

'If you're worried about privacy, why don't you

stay here instead of at the apartment block, then?' Brigitte offered.

'You'd be surprised at the number of fans of the show who would track me down wherever I stayed. I don't think your family, or Dad, needs people camped out the front of your house and I think you have enough on your plate without having a lodger who comes and goes at erratic hours.'

Brigitte shrugged. 'Dad wanders in the night. You could keep him company if you get in late from the hospital.'

A thought occurred to him. 'Do you need me to stay? Do you need an extra pair of eyes or hands?'

His sister shook her head. 'No, it's all right. It's enough that you're in town. This will give us time to make some decisions.'

'I'm sorry. I haven't been much help, have I? You and Kristin have shouldered the burden.'

'Kristin more than me,' Brigitte said. 'We've managed but it's getting harder. Dad is deteriorating and the timing is terrible with Kristin's baby due and my overseas study leave coinciding. We've got a few weeks up our sleeves but not much more than that. And unless you're planning on taking time off, we have to hope we get a bed for him somewhere soon. Anything else will just be a short-term fix.'

'How many options have we got?'

'Kristin and I have put his name on a couple of waiting lists but the trouble is we don't need just an ordinary bed, we need one in a dementia unit and we need a male bed. There aren't many beds allocated for men in nursing homes. Do you think you could pull any strings?' Brigitte asked.

'You'd have more luck than me, I reckon,' Caspar said. 'You're a local. I'm not one any longer.'

'But you're a celebrity and a medico—surely that counts for something.'

'I'll find out the names of the doctors who visit the nursing homes and maybe if they have visiting rights at the hospital too, I can have a word, but it's probably the nurse manager I need to sweet-talk. Why don't you give me the names of the nursing homes you've chosen and I'll see what I can do?'

Caspar knew he'd have to make an effort to

find a solution. It was time he did his share. This was something that had to be fixed, and soon.

Annie's weekend was dragging by. She'd done her ward rounds, been to a gym class with Tori, cleaned and done her grocery shopping. But buying meals for one didn't take long and now she was restless. Sunday afternoon stretched before her, she had the rest of the day to fill and no plans.

For the past few months she'd been content with her own company and going to work each day had been enough activity for her, but today she was bored. She checked her phone for the umpteenth time but she hadn't missed any calls. There wasn't one woman in labour who needed her help.

She pulled on her running shoes and decided to walk to the store. Surely a good movie could fill up a couple of hours. She shoved her phone, keys and wallet into a small bag and slung it across her body before heading out the door.

Of course, deciding to get out of the house was all it took to make her phone ring. She was halfway between home and the hospital when she took a call from Emergency. There had been a motor vehicle accident on Millicent Road. One of the victims was a pregnant woman and Tang, the RMO on duty, wanted Annie's expertise. The woman was being brought in by ambulance, they were still several minutes away, but all other details were sketchy. Annie could jog home and get her car but instead she turned and headed for the hospital.

Caspar heard the automatic doors of the emergency department slide open behind him. A hint of jasmine surrounded him and he knew Annie had arrived. He'd been keeping an eye out for her all weekend and had been surprised not to see her earlier, but there had been no babies born this weekend. He knew, he'd been checking.

Blue Lake Hospital served a large rural community but it still wasn't as busy as a city hospital and, on average, there were only two births a week.

He turned now, seeking her out, not doubting that she was there.

Annie was just inside the doors, her cheeks were flushed and she seemed out of breath. She was dressed in exercise gear, skintight Lycra leggings and a fitted tank top. Her legs were incredible and for a slightly built woman Caspar noticed she had curves in all the right places.

He saw her push her hair off her face and lean forward, placing her hands on her hips to catch her breath, giving him an unexpected glimpse of cleavage and a not totally unexpected stirring of desire.

But this was not the time or place. He knew she wasn't keen on having him in her hospital but he'd been pleased to learn she had finally signed the television network's consent forms. He hoped that working together the other day had started to create the foundations for a harmonious professional relationship, but he didn't want to jeopardise a promising start by complicating matters, and satisfying any physical needs he might have were a long way down his list of priorities at present. He knew he still had to win her trust.

'Are you all right?' he asked.

Annie straightened up when she heard his voice. She nodded. 'Just unfit,' she replied. Running to the hospital had required more effort than her regular gym class.

Over Caspar's shoulder she could see the camera crew and she realised that Caspar hadn't been called in; more than likely he had been here already. Just because she'd had a quiet weekend it didn't mean he had. She looked from the cameraman back to Caspar. His jaw was darkened by weekend stubble, accentuating both his square jaw and his masculinity and making him even more attractive. Annie forced herself to concentrate. She didn't need distractions.

'Have you been working?' She hadn't actually thought they would work on weekends.

'There have been a few interesting cases and we filmed Kylie and Paul's reunion yesterday. We had their permission to film Paul meeting his babies for the first time.'

Annie thought that would have been rather special and despite her misgivings about the television series being filmed in her hospital, she realised she hoped that the stories would cast the hospital in a positive light. Although she still wished she could ignore the fact that Caspar and his team were there. But before she felt obligated to say something nice she was interrupted by Tang, the RMO on duty. She latched onto his presence, relieved to have someone else to talk to.

'Tang, what can you tell me?' Annie asked as the young resident approached her.

'A car misjudged overtaking a logging truck. He clipped the back of the truck, flipped and rolled down an embankment.'

Annie winced. Accidents involving logging trucks weren't uncommon in this area and they were often nasty, with the occupants of the cars always coming off second best. Annie hated dealing with car-accident victims. It brought back memories of her marriage. Her husband's drink-driving conviction had been the final nail in the coffin of their relationship and now car accidents brought back old memories that she'd rather forget.

'The male driver is being airlifted to Adelaide with spinal injuries,' Tang continued, 'and his wife is on her way here. The driver of the truck is being treated for shock.'

'So, only one patient for us,' Annie remarked as they heard the sound of the ambulance siren approaching.

'Or maybe two,' Caspar said, 'depending on what's happening with the baby.'

'Let's hope we can keep it to one, then,' Annie replied, as the ambulance pulled into the bay.

The paramedics wasted no time in removing their patient from the ambulance. 'Unconscious female, eighteen weeks pregnant, BP eighty over fifty, possible pelvic fracture, but no other serious visible injuries.' The paramedics recited the information they knew.

'Her name is Suzanne.' Annie was aware of the camera hovering behind her but she had no time to worry about that now. She looked at the paramedic, querying how he had so much information from an unconscious patient. 'Her husband was conscious at the scene,' he explained.

Annie and Tang jogged beside the stretcher as Suzanne was wheeled into Emergency.

'We're going to need a CT scan,' Annie told

Tang as she pulled a gown over her gym clothes. 'Her hypotension could be indicative of internal bleeding and we need to check for pelvic fractures.'

Suzanne was wheeled into an examination room, swiftly transferred to a hospital bed and connected to various monitors.

'Run a unit of blood and cross-match blood type,' Tang instructed the nurses as they attached electrodes and hung the drip bag on the stand.

The room was crowded but the team worked smoothly, everyone knowing their job and their place. They needed to get Suzanne as stable as possible before moving her for the CT scan. There was no time or space to deal with the television cameras.

'You can't follow us,' Annie told Liam as they prepared to move Suzanne. 'You don't have the patient's permission to film her.' Annie had accepted the inevitable and had signed the consent forms for the network yesterday, but she knew her signature was only part of the necessary paperwork.

'You know we can get permission later.' Caspar didn't even bother to discuss it with her and she had neither the time nor the energy to debate the facts with him. She had to trust that they wouldn't use footage already taken without obtaining permission.

'If your crew get in our way I'm kicking them out,' she said, keen to have the last word for once as she turned her back, preparing to take Suzanne to X-Ray. Liam and Keegan would have to work around the medical staff.

The CT scan results weren't good. The pictures showed significant abdominal haemorrhaging and a fracture of the right acetabulum.

Suzanne was rushed to the operating theatre where Annie would have to do her best to stop the bleeding before the orthopod would take over. Tori was the anaesthetist on call, which Annie was pleased about, as she knew she didn't have to worry about that end of things. The theatre team continued to pump blood into their patient to counteract the haemorrhaging while Annie, Caspar and Tang all scrubbed, preparing for surgery.

Annie stood side by side with Caspar, both

with soap suds up to their elbows as they prepared to go into Theatre. She took a deep breath. Caspar was ready and willing to assist. If they were going to have any chance of saving Suzanne and the baby, she needed all the help she could get. Tang was capable but she doubted he'd had the experience needed for this scenario. She barely knew Caspar but they had worked together smoothly to deliver Kylie's twins just forty-eight hours ago and there was something about him that evoked a sense of capability.

An air of assuredness, confidence and calmness that made her feel she could trust him. She didn't like the feeling, that she was so willing to trust a man she barely knew, but she would have to. In this situation she had to believe he wouldn't let her down.

Annie backed through the door into the theatre. Tori had anaesthetised Suzanne and she was prepped, her body draped in sterile sheets, with the exception of her abdomen, which was stained orange by the antiseptic liquid. Her abdomen was distended but Annie knew that distension probably wasn't due to her pregnancy but was more than likely a result of intra-abdominal bleeding. She couldn't waste time. Gloved and gowned, with Caspar beside her and the camera crew forgotten in the background, Annie got to work.

But what she found when she opened Suzanne up wasn't what she'd expected.

It was worse. Much worse.

CHAPTER FOUR

'OH, MY GOD.' Annie could scarcely believe what she was seeing. The CT scan had shown a massive amount of blood in the abdominal cavity but it had been difficult to see where it was coming from. Now that Annie had opened Suzanne up they were able to see the extent of the damage.

Suzanne's uterus had ruptured too. Annie could see a large tear in the upper quadrant. The baby, a tiny boy, was lying outside the womb, marooned in Suzanne's abdomen. Annie's fingers ran along the umbilical cord, praying that her eyes were deceiving her. But she wasn't that lucky. The umbilical cord had ruptured.

Annie looked up at Caspar. Wanting him to tell her that it wasn't as bad as it looked. Wanting him to tell her it would be all right.

But of course he couldn't do that.

His green eyes locked onto hers. Annie could

see compassion in their depths but she could also see despair.

The baby was blue and lifeless.

'We can't save the baby.' Caspar told her what she already knew. His deep voice was husky and Annie knew this was affecting him as much as it was her. 'We have to try to save Suzanne.'

Caspar checked for vital signs but they both knew it was too late. He gently lifted the baby out of Suzanne. He was perfectly formed in miniature. Only about fourteen centimetres long, he was slightly bigger than the palm of Caspar's hand and his little head rested against Caspar's fingers. Caspar wrapped him in a small surgical drape before handing him to one of the nurses as Annie swallowed, trying in vain to dislodge the lump that had formed in her throat.

'Can you organise a heat lamp? I want to keep him warm and nearby.' Caspar spoke to the nurse. 'Suzanne may want to hold him when she wakes up but I don't want him placed where she can see him without asking. That might be too big a shock.'

The nurse nodded and Annie blinked back

tears. She had no idea what Suzanne would want but she was sure she wouldn't want to hear that her baby had died. At least Caspar had thought about what might come next.

The baby was so tiny. Annie knew he wouldn't weigh more than a couple of hundred grams and at eighteen weeks gestation he was too young to be considered a stillbirth, too young to legally require a name, too young to legally require registering. It was heartbreaking but she couldn't afford to waste time. She had to try and save Suzanne. The nurses were running another unit of blood as Suzanne continued to bleed heavily.

Annie continued to work, blocking out thoughts of the baby as she tried to stem the blood flow. She was almost on autopilot, her hands moving swiftly to cauterise damaged blood vessels. She could smell the burning tissue as she worked and she was aware of the constantly replaced bags of blood. She felt like she was fighting a losing battle but eventually the bleeding slowed as she sealed and repaired the vessels, and then she had to turn her attention to the torn uterine wall.

That took several more minutes but finally she

was able to stitch Suzanne's abdominal wound. The surgery would leave a scar that would resemble that of a Caesarean section but Suzanne would have no happy ending and Annie dreaded having to impart the news. She'd been able to save Suzanne's uterus, which she hoped might at least give her the chance of having children in the future, but Annie knew that wasn't going to lessen the pain right now.

And it wasn't over yet. Once Annie had finished, Suzanne was left in Tori's care as they waited for the orthopod to see what he could do about her fractured pelvis. But Annie didn't doubt that Suzanne would recover faster from her fractured pelvis than she would from her fractured heart.

A bassinette with a heat lamp had been brought into the theatre. The baby would be moved with Suzanne but kept out of sight, as Caspar had instructed. Annie wished the baby was out of sight now. She tried not to look at Suzanne's son as she left the OR but, of course, that was impossible. Her eyes were drawn to the tiny bundle and tears blurred her vision again. It was such a tragic situation.

She put her head down and headed for the scrub room, vaguely aware of Colin as he came into Theatre to take care of Suzanne's fractures. Annie couldn't imagine how Suzanne was going to bear the news that her husband was in another hospital hundreds of kilometres away and her baby was dead.

Annie flung open the door to the scrub room, pulled off her mask, gloves and cap and tossed them into the bin, before removing her gown. She leant against the sink, keeping her back turned to the window that looked into the OR. She closed her eyes and let the tears run down her face. She had a few moments of peace before she heard the door open as someone joined her. The air around her stirred and she smelt a faint scent of peppermint and she knew it was Caspar.

'Hey, what's the matter?'

She kept her eyes closed as his voice wrapped around her, calm and deep and soothing, and then she felt his arms wrap around her too, pulling her against his chest. He was warm and solid and smelt wonderful. Annie knew she should resist but she didn't have the energy. It was a comforting place to be. She felt safe and shielded from her troubled thoughts.

Caspar didn't hesitate when he found Annie in the scrub room, in tears and alone. Taking her in his arms felt natural. It was what he would do for his sisters if he found them upset.

Annie fitted perfectly against his chest and into the curve of his shoulder. She'd removed her cap and her hair fell down her back, forming a soft, smooth cushion for his hand as he pulled her into him.

But holding her in his arms felt nothing like hugging his sisters.

He tried to block that thought from his mind. Tried to convince himself that he was only doing what he'd do for anyone else. That Annie was no different to anyone else.

But she felt and smelt different. He couldn't deny that.

He felt her sobs begin to subside as he rubbed her back in a slow, circular rhythm to try and relax her. Her tears were soaking through his scrubs, turning the fabric damp and cool against his skin.

He knew how she felt. He hated it when he couldn't save a life. Losing a baby was devastating for everyone involved and he always found it difficult as it made him think of his own circumstances. Always made him wonder if his own birth mother had struggled with the decision to give him up. Made him wonder if she ever thought about what had happened to him. But he'd learnt not to dwell on that. It was all in the past. What mattered now was the present. What mattered now were Annie and Suzanne.

The door from Theatre opened and Caspar saw Liam, his camera propped on his shoulder, about to come into the room. He shook his head, shooing him away before Annie noticed his presence. She needed privacy and despite the fact that she'd consented to filming he knew she wouldn't thank him for this intrusion. He didn't want to bear the brunt of her ire if he let Liam film this scene.

Annie took her hands away from her face and let them fall to his chest. Two small, warm palms pressed against him and sent a surge of heat straight through his rib cage to his heart. His heart went into overdrive and heat flooded through his body, warming everything from his fingers to his toes. He could feel the warmth flowing in his bloodstream. He could feel a stirring of desire in the pit of his belly and a tightening in his groin. He had to remind himself to breathe. Focus.

He had to move her away. He couldn't let her feel the effect she had on him. He couldn't let her notice his reaction.

He stepped back, just half a pace, far enough for distance but still close enough that he could hold her as he wasn't willing to lose touch with her completely. 'Are you going to tell me what's wrong?'

She looked up at him. Her face was tear-stained and her eyes were shiny with unshed tears that were trapped against her lashes like dewdrops, threatening to spill over. The tip of her nose was red but somehow she still managed to look beautiful. It was incredible—he'd never known anyone who could look good while crying.

And then he knew he was in trouble. He had priorities: his dad; his job; the television series. He didn't have time for anything more. And Annie Simpson was definitely more.

The cold crept in as Caspar stepped away. Except for two warm spots on her upper arms where his hands still held her she felt as though her temperature had dropped several degrees. She looked up at him. Tall, dark and handsome, and just moments before she'd been in his embrace.

She couldn't believe she'd been in his arms. What had she been thinking? She needed to put him back into the box marked 'Do not open'. She couldn't believe she'd let him out. Let him close.

She was silently berating herself until she realised that *she* hadn't let him out. He'd taken himself out. He'd crossed her boundaries and entered her personal space.

But you welcomed him in, said the voice in her head. The voice she thought of as the voice of reason, only this time it wasn't being very reasonable. But it was right. Being in his arms had felt good. And she hadn't resisted. Even now her hands were still pressed against his chest, still touching him. She had to move away.

With great effort she removed her hands from his chest and, in order to try to make the movement seem natural, wiped her face, attempting to remove all traces of her tears. She rubbed her damp hands on her pants as she took a deep breath. That was a mistake. Another hit of peppermint assaulted her senses but it was enough to force her to concentrate.

She might not have resisted but she hadn't asked him for comfort. She hadn't asked him for empathy. Embarrassment and confusion made her angry. She was annoyed with herself and cross with him. She didn't care if they were both to blame. His gesture had taken her by surprise and, while she wasn't denying she felt better for it, she wasn't sure that his actions had been completely innocent.

Maybe his comfort had been genuine but perhaps he'd simply seen this as an opportunity to get past her defences, a chance to ingratiate himself into her good graces and make her more amenable to the idea of the television series.

She had no real idea but she decided she had enough to deal with without trying to second-guess Caspar's motives. The situation with Suzanne had left her emotionally spent and, given her lack of resistance, letting Caspar out of the box could only make matters worse. She'd have to be stronger. She'd have to make sure it didn't happen again. She needed to rebuild her barriers.

'You can't use that footage,' she snapped in response to his question.

A shadow darkened his eyes. He didn't answer immediately, just watched her.

Eventually he spoke. 'That's what's bothering you?'

Was that disappointment in his expression or was it just her imagination? She almost apologised for her mood. Almost.

'No one should have to watch that. It's too sad. Please tell me it's not something you would want to show your viewers?'

'I doubt very much we'd get permission from Suzanne to show that, and we won't ask.' He spoke slowly, his tone calm and measured, but Annie could hear the sadness in it too. 'I agree, it's not something people will want to watch. If we screen Suzanne's story, Gail will focus on the fact that we saved her life, *you* saved her life, she won't focus on the tragic loss of the baby.'

Annie may not have apologised but she did temper her irritation. It was difficult to stay angry when he was agreeing with her for once. It was difficult to stay angry while he was still holding her. His touch made it hard to concentrate. And she needed to concentrate. She needed to work out if she could trust him.

She had decided he could be trusted in the operating theatre but could he be trusted away from there? Could she trust him to put her patient before his viewers?

She really had no choice. She couldn't condemn him for something he hadn't yet done. She believed in people being innocent until proven guilty.

She would give him the benefit of the doubt.

Her tone was softer when she next spoke. 'Did you know Suzanne and her husband were driving here from Robe? They had an appointment

tomorrow for her eighteen-week antenatal ultrasound?'

He shook his head and she remembered he
hadn't been in the room when that information
had been passed onto her.

'She was coming here full of anticipation and
expectation and now all I have to give her is bad
news. Her husband is seriously injured, in a hospital hundreds of miles away, and she's lost the
baby.'

'You saved her life.'

'I'm not sure she'll thank me for that.'

'You did everything you could. I'm not denying it's going to be tough on her but she can't
blame you for anything.' He spoke softly, his
voice gentle and reassuring. 'If she's going to
blame anyone, she'll blame me. I'm the baby doctor. Suzanne was your patient and you did everything right for her. I couldn't save the baby,
I don't think anyone could have. Do you want
someone else to give her the news?'

Annie shook her head. 'No. It'll be okay.'

'Are you sure you're up to it? If you're this
upset you might not be the best person to have

this conversation with her. Do you want me to do it? I'll have to speak to her at some point.'

The thought of having that conversation with Suzanne made her feel sick but it was her job. A job she'd managed to do perfectly well before he'd arrived in town so why was she now letting him take her into his arms, letting him offer support? She didn't need it. She didn't need him. She needed to show him she could manage.

She was still sandwiched between him and the sink, his hands were still holding her arms and she'd made no effort to move away. She stepped around him, forcing him to let her go. She lifted her head. 'It's my job. I'll handle it.'

'She's going to be a while in Theatre yet so you'll have a long wait in front of you. Do you want me to give you a lift home?' He was still offering help. 'I can bring you back later when she wakes up.'

Annie shook her head. 'No, I'll wait in my office.'

She didn't want him to be nice to her. She felt like she'd let Suzanne down and she didn't want someone to make excuses for her. She straightened her shoulders and headed for the door before she was tempted to seek solace in his arms again. Before she was tempted to hide her face against his chest and let her sad thoughts float away. She couldn't depend on him. She didn't *want* to depend on him. She had no intention of depending on anyone except herself.

Annie might think she could cope with the situation but Caspar had no plans to let her deal with this alone. Not after finding her in tears. She hadn't asked him to go with her to talk to Suzanne but she couldn't keep him away altogether. He was worried about her. Since he'd met her he'd been trying to figure out what she wanted. Now it was obvious. She wanted a happy ending.

He almost smiled to himself. He should have been able to guess that. He'd had enough experience with women, and wasn't that what they all wanted? He knew he couldn't deliver the fairytale ending but surely he could think of a way to make her feel better. He couldn't fix the situation but surely he could improve it.

He needed a bit of luck and he got it when his producer called and handed him a solution.

Caspar swung into action. He felt much better now that he had a plan. He asked the nurses to call him as well when Suzanne woke up. He wasn't planning on seeing Suzanne but he didn't want to miss Annie.

He was waiting for her when she emerged from Recovery. It was a moment or two before she noticed him and he used that time to observe her unseen. Purple smudges under her eyes contrasted sharply with her pale skin and made her brown eyes look even darker than normal. Her pink lips were pressed together, drawn and pinched. She looked tired.

He saw her scan the corridor, saw her register his presence, and when her eyes met his he realised that the expression in her eyes wasn't tiredness, it was sadness. Caspar's heart felt like a lead weight in his chest. He longed to take her in his arms again, longed to offer comfort, but he knew it was unwise.

She hesitated and he wondered if she would approach him or not.

'How are you?' he asked. As far as questions went it was highly inadequate but it was all he could come up with. And he knew that if he didn't say something quickly he wouldn't be able to resist closing the distance between them and offering physical comfort.

Annie almost wasn't surprised to see Caspar standing in the corridor. She was beginning to get used to him popping up when she least expected it. For a moment she thought she might even have been glad to see him until she stopped to wonder why he was there. She hoped it wasn't because he wanted to film something. She wasn't in the mood for that. Not in the slightest.

But his question hadn't been about work. It had been about her. And he hadn't bothered asking how things had gone with Suzanne, which was a blessing. He must know how difficult that conversation would have been.

She was standing several feet from him, forcing herself to keep some distance. She shrugged in response to his question. She was exhausted, physically and emotionally, and she didn't have the energy to construct a sentence.

He didn't seem to expect an answer. 'We got the best outcome we could have,' he told her. 'You saved her life. There was nothing either of us could do for her son. Some days it's important to try to focus on what you did achieve, not on what you didn't.'

She knew he was right but it didn't make her feel any better. She felt as though she had the weight of the world on her shoulders.

'If you're up to it I think I have something that might cheer you up,' he said.

That surprised her. 'How could you? You barely know me and even I can't think of anything that would help.'

He wasn't going to be shut down. 'Gail called. She's got the first edit ready from filming on Friday. What we taped with Kylie and Paul and the twins, the delivery and their reunion in the nursery. I thought that might be something you'd like to see,' he persisted.

'Watching footage that I didn't want taken, you think that's going to cheer me up?'

He smiled at her. 'You're feeling better already, I see.'

'What do you mean?'

'You're arguing with me again.'

He was right, she realised, she did feel better. Having him there, someone who had gone through the drama with her, someone who understood what the day had been like, had lightened the burden of responsibility. And it didn't hurt that he was still smiling at her and he'd changed out of his scrubs into jeans that hugged his hips and an aqua T-shirt that moulded to his chest and made his eyes look more blue than green. Just looking at him was enough to lighten her mood.

'Please,' he said.

She hesitated.

'I'll drive you and drop you home afterwards,' he added, attempting to sweeten the deal, but that made her more hesitant. Not because she didn't want to go with him but because she did. But surely being in his tiny sports car would only complicate matters. He would be far too close for comfort. The memory of being in his arms was still so fresh.

She couldn't deny how good it had felt but it had left her feeling very confused. No, not confused, she knew exactly what she'd felt. Conflicted would be a better description, she thought. She didn't want to get close to Caspar, she didn't want to get close to anyone, but yet she'd let him close, she'd let him hold her, offer comfort—and she'd accepted. Without argument.

She could count on one hand the number of friends she'd made since moving to Mount Gambier. All right, she could count on one finger—Tori—and she knew it wasn't because the locals hadn't been welcoming. It was because she had shut them out. She hadn't made an effort.

She had promised herself she would keep away from Caspar but she'd fallen at the first hurdle. Found herself trusting him when other people had to earn her trust the hard way.

Her life had been nothing but complicated, her history messy, and trusting people didn't come easily to her. In her experience people almost always had an ulterior motive. Very few people really did things out of the goodness of their hearts without any thought for themselves.

'You don't have a car here, remember,' he said, still trying to convince her.

She could have postponed the invitation, delayed it until she had her own transport, but her misgivings weren't enough to overrule her hormones. She didn't feel like going home to an empty house. Going with Caspar was a far more appealing option.

CHAPTER FIVE

AN APPEALING OPTION, certainly, but not the most sensible one, she thought as she strapped herself into the seat beside him. The car smelt of leather. Caspar smelt of peppermint.

The car was tiny. Caspar was not.

The seats were soft, plump and comfortable. Caspar was masculine, lean and made her feel decidedly uncomfortable.

But it was too late now, she thought as he put the car into gear and pulled away from the hospital. She tried to blend into the upholstery, not sure if she wanted to be seen in his car as she tried to regain control of her nerves. She kept her face turned away from the window, not wanting to make eye contact with anyone on the street, but her plan wasn't a good one. The interior of the car was small, which meant there wasn't a lot to look at besides Caspar.

His posture was relaxed, making him seem at one with the car, as though the car was an extension of him, sleek and powerful. The engine noise was deep and rich and the car throbbed beneath her like a living thing, exacerbating the tension she was experiencing.

The lines of his jaw were darkened by his weekend stubble and Annie closed her eyes and imagined the contrast between the roughness of his beard and the softness of the leather seats under her hand.

She opened her eyes; after all, reality might be easier to handle than fantasy. Her gaze landed on the steering wheel; Caspar's fingers were looped casually around the curve, caressing the leather. Annie could remember how his fingers had felt on her arms, how his touch had warmed her skin, and her earlier nervousness doubled, churning through her stomach. She dragged her gaze away from Caspar, away from his long fingers, green eyes and designer stubble, and forced herself to look around the car. But, short of opening the glove box and searching through its contents, there wasn't an awful lot to hold her interest. Not when Caspar sat mere inches away.

'It's a very nice car,' she said, attempting to make conversation. 'The television network must pay you well.' She'd been trying desperately to find something to say and she could have kicked herself for the words that had popped out of her mouth, but it was too late.

'That's the second time you've mentioned my salary. Does it bother you, the idea that the network would pay me?' His eyes didn't leave the road and Annie couldn't tell if she'd annoyed him or not.

She remembered when she'd asked him how much he got paid. She remembered that he hadn't answered because she'd apologised and stopped him.

Did it bother her? She supposed it must do.

'It's the idea that people will do things differently if they're getting paid,' she admitted. 'People have been known to do strange things for money.'

Herself included. She had signed the consent forms for the television series because she needed to keep her job. Because she needed the money. If her divorce hadn't left her almost bankrupt she would have behaved very differently, she wouldn't even be in Mount Gambier. She knew exactly how money, or the lack of it, made people behave out of character.

Money was a big consideration for her but she hoped she wouldn't, or couldn't, be persuaded to do things she felt uncomfortable about just because she was being financially rewarded. And while she knew other people were often tempted by monetary gain, she hoped Caspar wasn't among them. She wanted him to be motivated by something other than money.

She realised that was unfair of her. After all, her move to Mount Gambier had been partly motivated by the lower cost of living in the country, which meant she'd be able to rebuild her life more quickly. But she was providing a necessary service, she wasn't using other people's situations to build up her bank account, and she hoped Caspar's reasons for doing the show weren't purely mercenary. He'd shown her such compassion today that she didn't want to be disappointed in him.

She shouldn't care. But she did.

'I couldn't agree with you more,' Caspar replied.

'What?'

'I think you're right. Money can do strange things to people. But I'm not doing this for the money. The network doesn't pay me, they're just filming me doing my job. If they paid me they would have to pay all of you. They do, however, make a generous donation to a children's charity on my behalf.'

'So you do the series for nothing?' Annie didn't know what to make of that information. On one hand she was pleased to hear that money wasn't his driving force but why would he choose to work under the watchful eye of television cameras? He must have something to gain from it.

'I agreed to be part of series one because I thought it was a chance to raise awareness of different medical conditions and ultimately I hoped to get the government to fund more health care programmes and initiatives. There are still so many underfunded areas.

'And,' he said as he pulled into the car park at the rear of the building that housed the local television station, 'if it makes you feel any better, I'm off the clock right now.'

It did make her feel a little better, Annie thought as she shut the car door. His offer to spend this time with her had come from him. It didn't mean that his reasons were necessarily purely unselfish but it was nice to know it had been his idea.

The television station was a small, unimaginative building painted an unattractive grey with lots of television aerials and satellite dishes on the roof. Caspar held the door open for her as they entered, and stopped to sign them in as Annie glanced around. There was a short corridor lined by several closed doors but she didn't see another soul.

'Where is everyone?' she asked. She hadn't stopped to consider that they'd be alone once they reached their destination. She'd thought there'd be safety in numbers.

Caspar gestured for her to follow him as he replied. 'Gail has gone, but she left everything set up for me. The local team will be preparing for the evening news broadcast so we're not in anyone's way.'

That wasn't what she'd been worried about. But she was being silly. Just because her hormones had gone into overdrive and she was nervous about being alone with him, it didn't mean anything would happen. After all, he couldn't possibly be attracted to her. Why on earth would he be? She was sure he had his pick of beautiful women, she'd seen plenty of them photographed with him, so why would he look twice at her?

He led her to a small viewing room. A desk, its surface covered with various hi-tech boxes and monitors, ran along one wall. Several screens were fixed to the wall above it and three chairs were crammed together in front.

Caspar pulled out a chair for her, before sitting down himself. He flicked some switches and pressed a few buttons and the overhead lights dimmed and one of the screens came to life. It wasn't a large one and Caspar pulled his chair closer to hers so they were both sitting in front of it. They were separated by only a few centimetres.

Annie tucked her feet under her chair so that their knees didn't touch but she could feel the heat coming off his body. She was still wearing her exercise gear and her arms were bare, the hairs standing to attention. The air felt charged, full of static, and while it could have come from all the electrical equipment in the room, Annie knew it didn't. It was coming from Caspar, almost as though he was positively charged and was seeking out her negative one.

Her nipples hardened, pushing against the Lycra of her tank top, obvious to anyone who cared to look. She crossed her arms over her chest and made herself concentrate on the screen.

A shot of Kylie came into focus, with the back of Annie's head in the foreground. The scene began with the discussion about where to deliver the babies—in Emergency or Maternity—before cutting to footage of Kylie being wheeled along the corridors.

Annie would swear that the footage had been speeded up, making everyone appear as though they were hurrying, and then suddenly the first twin was being delivered. Everything looked far more urgent and exciting than it had actually been. Annie was riveted to the screen. If Gail had managed to capture her attention like this through clever editing then Annie knew the audience would be even more entranced. Which was the whole idea.

Annie almost forgot about Caspar sitting beside her as she waited to see what happened next.

Liam had captured a lot of close-ups. Kylie cuddling the first twin and looking contented. Caspar holding the second twin and looking drop-dead gorgeous. The camera devoured Caspar, his colouring and the angles of his face were made to be photographed.

There was some footage of Annie but mostly it was of the back of her head, as she'd requested, except for a few frames where Liam had captured shots of her in profile when she had been handing the first twin to Caspar. She had a dreamy, slightly vacant expression on her face and she knew the shot had been taken just after she and Caspar had touched for the first time and she'd had been completely disoriented by the powerful charge his touch had sent through her.

Fortunately it looked like Annie was focussed on the baby when she knew the reality was that she hadn't been able to drag her gaze away from Caspar. She wanted to ask for that scene to be cut but she realised that would be ridiculous, That shot needed to be there. It was part of the story and the story was about Kylie's experience, not about her.

The actual delivery of the twins was only a small part of the edited version. Most of the scenes concentrated on Kylie and Paul's reunion and on Paul meeting his babies for the first time. Caspar featured prominently while she only appeared as an extra.

'What do you think?' Caspar asked as the screen went black.

'It's been really well edited,' she admitted. And it had certainly managed to distract her from the events that occurred earlier in the day. Which had been his intention.

Caspar pressed a button and the overhead lights came back on. 'And not too much footage of you?' He was smiling at her, looking his usual confident, handsome self. Assured of the answer.

'Not too much,' she agreed.

'Can we leave you in?'

Annie nodded.

'And future episodes? Are you still willing to be a part of those too?'

'I don't want to feature,' she told him, 'but if they're going to be presented like that then I'm happy to co-operate.'

She didn't want the camera's focus to be on her but she realised now, after seeing the footage, that it wasn't going to be about her. The hospital could do with the money the network had promised and she needed to be a team player.

'Excellent. Shall we go and grab a drink to celebrate our agreement?'

He wanted to go out? In public? She couldn't do that. That would be crossing more boundaries than she was prepared for. No matter how well intentioned his invitation was, anything more than a working relationship wasn't something she was going to encourage or accept. Being a team player didn't extend to social activities. Caspar had to stay in that box marked 'Do not open'.

'I'm not really dressed for it,' she replied, gesturing at her outfit. A flicker of what she took for disappointment in his eyes had her lifting the lid on the imaginary box. Just a tiny bit. After all his efforts today she felt she probably owed him something more than a refusal. 'You did offer to drop me home. I can make you a coffee there if you like,' she offered.

Caspar thought Annie looked perfectly fine in her gym gear, better than fine actually, but he happily accepted her alternative invitation. He'd won round one. He'd got her to agree to be part of the series and she seemed to have lowered her guard a little. She hadn't argued with him for the best part of fifteen minutes and had even invited him for coffee. Progress had been made.

Annie directed him to an old house on the outskirts of town. It sat squarely in the middle of a large block and was surrounded by aging fruit and citrus trees. It looked much too big for one person yet he had the impression she lived alone. The back of the house was almost smothered by a jasmine creeper and Caspar knew he'd never be able to smell the scent of jasmine without thinking of her.

She entered the house via the back door, which led directly into the kitchen, which appeared to be in almost original condition. Narrow cupboards with laminated bench tops lined two walls, the stove was tucked into the old fireplace and a large kitchen dresser took up most of the fourth wall. In the centre of the room was a laminated table, the type usually seen in institutions, and four vinyl chairs.

A shiny, modern, state-of-the-art coffee machine sat on the bench, looking completely out of place.

The 1950s décor was not at all what he had expected and was vastly different from what he was used to. Home for him was a stylish penthouse in an exclusive apartment block. Walking into Annie's kitchen was like stepping back in time, back to his boarding-school dining-hall days.

'Is this your house?' he asked.

'No, I'm renting,' she told him as she pushed a pile of paint colour charts to one end of the Formica kitchen table, dumping her bag on top of the mess. 'It came furnished,' she added, as she saw him taking it all in.

'With everything bar the coffee machine, I'm guessing.'

Annie nodded. 'And my bed. My landlord has been modernising the house.'

'While you're living in it?' He knew he'd never have the patience to live in the midst of renovations, no matter how minor.

'It's a little bit inconvenient but because of work I'm not here during the day so the tradesmen and I don't really get in each other's way. And it's kept the rent low. The kitchen is the last room on the list. The rest of the house isn't stuck in the same time warp any more,' she said, as she scooped freshly ground coffee into the machine. 'Have a seat, I'm just going to ring the hospital to check on Suzanne.'

'All good?' Caspar asked when she finished the call. He knew neither of them expected any more bad news. The hospital would have called Annie if necessary.

'She's sedated,' she replied, 'and her vitals are

stable so it appears as though we stopped the bleeding.'

'So are you feeling better about things now?'

'I feel better about the television series and about Suzanne, but I don't feel so good about her baby,' she said, as she passed him his coffee and set milk and sugar on the table.

She picked up an old, faded, pink sloppy joe that was hanging on the back of the chair and shrugged into it before she sat down. The neck had stretched, allowing one shoulder to slip down, revealing her collarbone and the curve of her deltoid muscle at the top of her arm.

She was wearing more than she had been a moment before yet Caspar had a sense that he was glimpsing forbidden skin. The idea was tantalising and caused him to lose his train of thought. He forced himself to stir his coffee, which was unnecessary as he took it plain and black but it gave him a chance to recover his equilibrium. He was careful with his words.

'Losing a patient is always difficult. Are there any support networks in town for family and staff to access if they need to?'

'I would imagine so but I'm not sure.'

He was a little surprised that Annie didn't know the answer. 'What have you done in the past?'

'I haven't lost a patient, mother or baby, in the six months I've been here,' she explained. 'High-risk pregnancies are sent to Adelaide or Melbourne in plenty of time, and after today I'm going to make sure that practice continues. Today was not something I'm keen to repeat in a hurry.'

It wasn't something she *ever* wanted to repeat. Caspar had told her to focus on what she had been able to achieve but she knew it would be a long time before she could forget the sight of that tiny baby, still and lifeless, cradled in Caspar's palm.

She had no idea how she was going to get to sleep tonight and if there hadn't been the chance she'd be called back to the hospital she would have suggested they drink something stronger than coffee. But coffee it was, she thought as she drained her cup.

She placed it on the table at the same moment as Caspar. The table was so small that her fingers brushed the backs of his knuckles as he put his cup beside hers. Annie froze, paralysed by the surge of awareness that made her stomach tremble and her heart race. She felt a stirring in the air as the heat left Caspar's body and rushed through hers.

She lifted her head to find him watching her. His eyes were dark green, darker than she'd ever seen them, and she could see herself reflected in their depths. Neither of them moved a muscle. Annie wasn't sure she was even breathing.

Movement in the corner of the kitchen caught her eye, startling her, and it was enough to break the bubble of attraction in which she found herself. She pulled her hand back and exhaled through slightly parted lips, turning to face the very pregnant cat that had just sneaked in through the open back door.

'Aggie, have you come for a feed?' she said.

'Yours?' Caspar queried. 'Are you constantly surrounded by pregnant females?'

Annie laughed as she stood up and closed the back door. Aggie had provided her with the perfect reason to move out of Caspar's force field and she was relieved to find she could still walk and talk and breathe.

'She's not mine. She belongs to Bert, my landlord. He lives next door but Aggie knows I'm a soft touch. I'm thinking of keeping one of her kittens when they're ready for a new home.'

Speaking of Bert made her realise that aside from her octogenarian landlord and neighbour, Caspar was the only man she had invited into her house. While Bert had almost blended into the furnishings Caspar was a complete contrast. He was too big, too vibrant, too virile to be contained within these four walls. It had been a mistake to invite him here. She wasn't keeping her distance at all. She had well and truly opened the box. She hoped it wasn't too late to stuff him back inside.

'Are you planning on staying in Mount Gambier?' he asked.

'I might. I'm only on contract but it would be nice to settle down somewhere for a while,' she said as she poured some cat food into a small bowl and placed it on the floor.

'Have you moved a lot?'

She nodded but didn't volunteer any further information.

'Well?'

'Well, what?'

'Why have you moved so much? Was it work? It sounds interesting.'

'It's not,' she replied, as she decided what to tell him. She figured she could give him an edited version. 'I moved a lot as a child.'

'Because of your parents' work?'

'Not exactly. My mother was a nurse and my father was a carpenter with a rather erratic employment record. My parents had a rather volatile relationship, not helped by my father's inconsistent employment. He worked on construction sites, sometimes for the mining companies, sometimes in small towns, wherever he could find a job.

'My mother would follow him around the country for periods of time, dragging me with her, but we never seemed to stay permanently. Inevitably things would play out the same way over and over again. Construction work would dry up or finish and my father would be "between jobs". He'd then spend his spare time at the pub, which led to fighting, which would lead to my mother saying she wasn't going to put up with it any more and she'd pack our bags and we'd leave.'

'Where did you go?'

'Back to my gran's, my mum's mum. But that would only be temporary too. Dad would eventually get a job and beg Mum to come back. She was never able to resist him. I never understood what was happening. I still can't figure it out, but Mum always said that even though most of the time she was miserable with him, she was more miserable without him.'

'How often did you move?'

'Sometimes every few months. I don't think we ever stayed in one place for more than a year,' she said, as she closed up the bag of cat food and put it back under the sink. 'It's not the way I'd want anyone to grow up, never knowing where you were going to be from one minute to the next. Being taken away from people without notice. Never having anywhere to call home.'

'And you did this until you started university?'

'No, only until I was twelve.'

'What happened then?'

'My parents died in a house fire.'

She heard his intake of breath. She'd shocked him. She hadn't meant to but she wasn't sure why she'd been so blunt. If she ever shared that information with anyone, she was usually a little more subtle.

'Annie, I'm so sorry. Were you there?'

She hadn't meant to pause, she hadn't wanted to give him an opportunity to offer any sympathy or to ask questions. She hadn't meant to do a lot of things but Caspar seemed to have the ability to throw her off kilter.

She nodded. 'I'd been asleep but something woke me and our neighbour said he found me in the hall. He managed to get me out but he couldn't get into my parents' room. The fire had started there and by the time the fire brigade got to us it was too late. I was the only survivor.'

'Were you the only other person in the house? No siblings?'

'I'm an only child. Whenever we were going to or from Dad's place Mum always said she couldn't imagine dragging more kids around.'

'Were you hurt?'

'Not physically. I suffered from PTSD and lost my capacity for speech for about three months. There was an investigation into the fire and the media became fascinated with the case and with me because I wasn't speaking. That was my first experience with the media.'

'As a twelve-year-old after a traumatic event?'

She nodded.

'I can see why you don't like to be followed by cameras.'

She didn't tell him that for a long time she hadn't actually been able to remember the events of that night and had been placed into foster-care for three nights because her gran, her only other relative, was living interstate and, because she herself hadn't been talking, it had taken some time to track her down.

Annie wasn't volunteering any more information and Caspar didn't ask more questions about the fire. His thoughts had moved ahead. 'Where did you live after the fire?'

'With my gran. Her house was the only place I've ever felt at home.' It was the only place where

Annie had felt truly safe and loved, and she knew she longed to re-create that feeling in a house of her own one day.

'What happened to her?'

He was watching her closely and she knew he was wondering how she could have left the only place she truly loved.

'Gran died and I had to sell the house.' She phrased her words carefully, deliberately making it sound as though her gran had died recently and that selling the house was linked to her gran's death when, in fact, her gran had died nine years ago while she had still been at university, before Annie had embarked on her ill-fated marriage. The marriage that had cost her the house.

He didn't need to know she'd had to sell the house to pay her husband's fines. That his drink-driving conviction had meant his insurance had been null and void and that the consequences of his actions had cost her her home. When her gran had died she had lost the person who had loved her most in the world. She had tried to replace her with a husband and then to lose her home as well had almost been the end for her.

But that was a whole different story and not one she was prepared to tell Caspar. She was trying to move on from there and her move to the country was part of the healing process. She was seeking a new start.

'Do you have other family? Aunts, uncles, cousins?'

Annie shook her head. 'No, there's only me.' It was time to change the topic of conversation. She didn't want to sound depressed or maudlin. 'We'll have to talk about your family instead. Do they all still live around here?'

Caspar nodded. 'Dad and my sisters are here.'

'Do you visit often?'

'No. That was one reason I pushed for the show to be filmed here when the network was looking for alternative hospitals.'

'Filming here was your idea?' Annie was surprised. Along with the box marked 'Do not open', she'd also put him in a box labelled 'Hotshot, big-city doctor'. She knew she was being unfair. She'd judged him on his celebrity status, his car and his impeccably tailored suits, even though his behaviour had been anything but flashy.

'Dad suffers from dementia,' he explained. 'I've been letting my sisters handle it for too long. I thought it was time I did my bit. Filming the series here meant I could help out.'

'Is your dad in care?'

'No.' Caspar shook his head. 'He's living with one of my sisters but we need to look at other options. He's declining rapidly.'

'Why didn't you just take holidays? Surely you didn't have to move the whole series here?' she asked.

Caspar shrugged. 'I prefer to be busy.'

Annie imagined that looking for a suitable nursing-home bed would have kept him very busy but that was just her opinion. It didn't make her right. 'Are you staying with one of your sisters?'

'No. The network has put us into apartments near the lake. But my sister, Brigitte, feeds me most nights.' Caspar paused and Annie could see in his eyes as his thoughts took a different direction. He checked his watch. 'Which reminds me, I'm late for dinner. Again,' he said as he stood up. 'I should go. If I don't mend my ways, she'll stop offering to feed me.'

For a split second Annie thought about inviting him to stay for dinner with her. But then common sense prevailed. She could stretch her dinner for one to feed a second female but she doubted she'd have enough to satisfy a male appetite.

And why would he want to stay anyway? Thinking about her gran made her realise how often she was lonely and how much she missed company, but Caspar wasn't the answer. He should go.

'Thanks for the coffee.' He'd crossed the kitchen floor and was standing in front of her now. Annie had the kitchen sink behind her and she thought back to the last time they'd been in this same position only a few hours earlier. It seemed a lifetime ago.

Her eyes were level with his chest and she watched it rise and fall as he breathed. If she lifted her hand she'd be able to place it over his heart, she'd be able to feel him breathe. The pull of attraction was back. Annie could feel herself fixed within his force field and she made herself keep her hands by her sides. Out of danger's way.

He reached towards her and Annie held her

breath, waiting to see what he was going to do. He bent his head and she lifted her face up and met his eyes.

CHAPTER SIX

'ARE YOU GOING to be all right by yourself?' he asked.

His hand was past her shoulder now. He wasn't reaching for her, she realised, he was reaching for the doorknob. Disappointment flooded through her, dousing the warm glow in her belly with cold reality. 'Yes, of course,' she answered. She was used to being on her own. She didn't always like it but she was used to it.

He paused and for a moment Annie thought he had something more to say. But then he turned the doorknob and let himself out into the night.

Annie shut the door and leant against it. She closed her eyes as she tried to make sense of the myriad emotions swamping her. Desire, disappointment, relief and loneliness all competed for space in her head.

Loneliness won, shrouding her in its icy grip,

emphasising the emptiness of the room. The warmth that had come from having someone to share a drink with, a conversation with, had gone with Caspar.

Loneliness was an ache in the pit of her stomach.

But she knew the cure. She'd had plenty of practice.

Keep busy.

She took their coffee cups to the sink to rinse them. The cat wound her plump, furry body between Annie's calves as if she sympathised with Annie's predicament. The phone rang as she dried the second cup.

'Would you like to tell me what's going on? I've been trying to reach you all afternoon.' Tori's voice came down the line.

'I've been busy.'

They both knew Annie was never busy except when she was at work.

'I could see that.' Down the line Annie could hear the smile in Tori's voice. As the anaesthetist Tori would have had a bird's-eye view of Annie being wrapped in Caspar's arms. 'What I want to know is just what is it the two of you have been busy doing. If you've been ignoring me because you've been having wild sex all afternoon, that's okay, but I'm not interested in any other excuse.'

Annie had ignored several calls from Tori. She knew she wasn't ignoring anything urgent because important calls regarding patients would come through the hospital switchboard, not through Tori's mobile.

'Sorry to disappoint you,' she replied. 'He took me to see the first edit of the footage they've taken so far. That's it.' Annie wasn't ready to share anything more than that. Besides, what was there to share? Nothing had happened.

'So he's not with you now?'

'No.'

'I'm coming over. I'll pick up a movie and you can make up a story about your afternoon of steamy sex to keep me entertained.'

Annie knew there was no point in trying to put Tori off. She'd be around regardless, but at least that would take care of the loneliness.

Annie didn't know whether to be relieved or disappointed when a few days passed with very little

contact with Caspar. Tori kept checking for updates but there was absolutely nothing to report.
No babies had been born and she'd had no cases
that had been considered interesting enough for
the cameras and nothing exciting was happening with Kylie or Suzanne to warrant any further screen time.

She had bumped into Caspar during ward
rounds but there had been nothing they'd needed
to discuss and there had been no need to call for
his services. She'd seen him being interviewed
by the one of the entertainment channels outside
the hospital and his photo had been in the local
newspaper *again*, but that just served to remind
her of their differences. He was happy being in
the public eye while she would do anything to
avoid the attention.

On top of all that she was a little embarrassed
that she'd confided her family history to him *and*
then had thought he had been going to kiss her.
And that she'd wanted him to. She decided she
couldn't blame him if he was avoiding her.

But just as she was aware that their paths
weren't crossing so she was aware of her days

passing slowly. Whereas she'd been happy with the routine days and lack of drama that she'd experienced since moving to the country, she now found herself wishing for a little more excitement. And Caspar St Claire had the potential to give her excitement in spades.

But, she reminded herself, Caspar St Claire wasn't for her. She was managing just fine on her own.

Annie had one more patient to see before lunch and then she'd be free to think about any topic she chose, but for now she owed it to her patient to concentrate. She picked up the referral letter on her desk. As she reread the letter she remembered a phone call she'd had in regard to this patient earlier in the week.

Taylor Cartwright was a sixteen-year-old schoolgirl who thought she was pregnant by her teenage boyfriend. She was coming to the appointment with her high-school principal, Mrs Brigitte Lucas, who had organised the referral through a medical contact and had phoned Annie to give her some background. According to Mrs Lucas, Taylor was from a very religious family and Taylor didn't want to say anything to her parents until she knew for sure what her situation was.

Annie thought it strange that she would confide in her school principal and not her own family, but she would reserve her judgement until she met them both and got a feel for the case.

Annie finished getting the background straight in her head before calling them through to her office.

Taylor was a reasonably tall girl with a healthy, solid build. Because of her larger frame Annie knew Taylor could be many weeks pregnant before anyone would notice major physical changes.

'I assume you've missed a period or two or had some very light spotting?' Annie asked the teenager. 'Have you done a home pregnancy test?'

'Yes. Mrs Lucas gave me one. I couldn't get one from the pharmacy because someone might have seen me and told my mum.'

This seemed a bit above and beyond her idea of the job description of a high-school principal. Annie looked enquiringly at the headmistress.

'We run a programme at my high school for

teenage mums. It allows them to finish their schooling around the demands of a baby. The girls know they can come to me for support,' Brigitte explained.

'The test was positive?'

Taylor nodded.

'I'll do another test, just to confirm that, and once we know for sure we can talk about your options,' Annie said. 'Do you remember when your last menstrual cycle started?'

'Mrs Lucas told me you'd ask that,' Taylor said, and told Annie the date.

Annie sent Taylor into the bathroom to give a urine sample while she calculated dates and asked Brigitte some more questions.

'Do you have many teenage mothers finishing their schooling?' In the six months Annie had been working at the hospital she hadn't, to her knowledge, encountered any pregnant girls who were still at school and neither had she met Brigitte Lucas.

'Fortunately, not too many,' Brigitte replied. 'There are four who have had their babies and are trying to finish their schooling and only Taylor, as far as I know, who is pregnant now. Not all of the girls need my input to the same degree as Taylor. Most have family support eventually, but I think it's important for them to know that there is help and that completing their education is an option. It might take a year or two longer than they'd planned but in my experience it can make all the difference to their futures.'

Annie couldn't imagine trying to juggle the demands of motherhood with finishing high school but she guessed she was way past having to worry about that. She was more worried that she'd never have a family of her own. She didn't want to be a single mother. She wanted the fairy-tale, she wanted to meet Mr Right and then have a family. With her family history there was no way she'd contemplate trying to do it alone. But the closer she got to thirty the more she thought it might not happen for her.

However, she couldn't worry about that now, she thought as Taylor finished in the bathroom.

'Positive,' Annie said as she tested Taylor's sample. 'You're having a baby.'

Taylor blanched and Annie was glad she'd

waited until the teenager was sitting down. Despite her earlier positive test, it was clear that Taylor had been hoping that perhaps it had been wrong, and she clearly had misgivings.

Annie watched as Brigitte reached across and held Taylor's hand. 'Two positives tests. It looks like this is really happening for you.'

Taylor met Brigitte's eyes and Annie was relieved to see her straighten her shoulders. She might have wished the news were different but she at least appeared to have some strength of character.

'What's next?' Brigitte asked Annie, as Taylor's gaze swung over to her.

Annie smiled at the girl. 'There are lots of decisions to make and things to discuss, but first I think we should have a look at your baby.'

'I can see it?' Taylor's voice wobbled slightly but she wasn't denying the truth and Annie took that as a positive sign.

'I can do an ultrasound scan. It's a non-invasive technique that uses sound waves to give us a picture of your baby. It will help me to determine or confirm dates too,' Annie replied. The scan would also allow her to check that everything was as it should be at this stage.

When Taylor was comfortable on the examination bed Annie quickly checked her blood pressure before squeezing the conducting gel onto her stomach and sweeping the transducer head backwards and forwards to build up a picture of the baby.

She found the amniotic sac and inside it was a tiny foetus. There was no mistaking the little jellybean shape.

'There's your baby,' Annie said. 'Two arms, two legs,' she said as she pointed to the screen. 'It all looks about right for ten weeks gestation. See the little flicker, like an anemone opening and closing? That's your baby's heart.'

'Wow, that is so cool. It's a little person already.'

'So, this is good news?' Brigitte asked the teenager.

'I don't know about good but I do know that I am going to keep it. I can't believe I have a little person inside me.'

'What about the baby's father?' Annie asked,

as she printed off a picture for Taylor and cleaned up the gel. 'Does he know?'

Taylor shook her head as she stared at the black and white photo of her baby. 'Not yet. But I'll have to tell him.' She hesitated slightly before adding, 'And my parents.'

Annie hoped Taylor would be supported through this, at least by her parents and hopefully her boyfriend too, but she knew there was little she could do about that.

'You have some important decisions to make,' Annie said, as Taylor hopped up from the examination table. 'And when you've had time to tell the baby's father and your parents the news, I'd like you to make an appointment to see me and bring anyone who would like to support you. I'm sure everyone will have questions.

'There's no hurry to come back to me. Everything is perfectly natural and normal and healthy, but if you have any concerns at any stage, let me know. And at some point we will have to have a conversation about safe sex. Not just to prevent pregnancy but to protect against sexually transmitted diseases too.'

Taylor went bright red when Annie broached that topic. Annie was always amazed that teenagers were embarrassed about having that discussion yet weren't embarrassed about the fact that they'd clearly been having unprotected sex. But she wasn't going to lecture Taylor today. Instead, she spent several more minutes answering Taylor's immediate questions before she gathered a pile of brochures and handed them to the teenager.

'There's some useful information here, plus a number for a good social worker if you would like someone else to talk to.'

Annie expected to find an empty waiting room as she escorted Brigitte and Taylor to the door of her office so she was surprised to find someone standing there, and even more surprised to see it was Caspar. She was definitely not expecting him.

Automatically she put a hand to her head, checking to see if her hair was a mess or whether she looked presentable. As she chastised herself for being so vain she noticed Taylor doing a double-take when she spied Caspar.

Despite the fact that Caspar was old enough to be Taylor's father, Annie noticed that even teenagers weren't immune to his good looks. She smiled to herself. The poor girl was being swamped with hormones. Was it any wonder she was affected by Caspar? Annie didn't imagine many women would be completely unaffected. The only one who didn't seem fazed was Brigitte.

She walked straight up to him and hugged him, and Annie was surprised to feel a surge of jealousy.

'Hey, little brother, are you looking for me?'

Brigitte was Caspar's sister? Annie looked closely at the two of them, searching for a family resemblance, but apart from a similar determination about them they were like chalk and cheese to look at. Brigitte was fair while Caspar was dark. She had blue eyes, not green, and she had none of his height.

'If I were, I wouldn't be looking here,' Caspar replied, smiling. 'I'm looking for Annie.'

He fixed his eyes on her. 'I know you've a lunch break scheduled—have you got time to grab a bite to eat? There's something I'd like to discuss with you.'

Annie felt herself flush. Even though she knew it would be work related, just the idea of Caspar inviting her to lunch made her heart pound and her colour rise. She seriously needed to get a grip.

She nodded, before saying goodbye to Brigitte and Taylor and reminding Taylor about her follow-up appointment.

'You had something you wanted to discuss with me?' Annie asked the moment they had chosen their lunch and a seat.

Caspar had purposely chosen a semi-secluded table in the corner of the cafeteria. He knew people would assume they were discussing work and, while that was his intention, he didn't want to be overheard if their discussion took a change in direction. But it seemed Annie was treating this lunchtime break purely as a professional one.

He nodded. 'I saw Kylie Jones this morning when I was checking the twins. She says you are planning on discharging her.'

'Tomorrow,' Annie agreed. 'There's no medical reason to keep her in hospital.'

'I realise that but I thought you might want an update on the twins. They need to gain another hundred grams each and preferably do that without any losses in between before I'll be happy to send them home.'

'Kylie can come into the hospital each day to be with the twins until they are ready for discharge. I can't justify a bed for her,' Annie replied. She took a sip of her coffee before she added, 'You didn't need to have lunch with me to discuss this.'

Her comment made him smile. He wondered if she was always so prickly or whether he brought out her defensive streak.

'Maybe I wanted to have lunch with you,' he said, surprising himself with his honesty and hoping it didn't make her run for shelter.

He had deliberately kept his distance for the past few days as he'd tried to work out how he felt about her. Annie Simpson unsettled him. She fascinated him. She excited him. Her forceful opinions intrigued him and it wasn't often that people disagreed with him so vehemently or so delightfully. He wasn't used to being amused when people disagreed with him yet her unexpected comments constantly made him smile.

But despite her strong opinions he sensed a fragility about her. Initially he'd thought her delicate appearance had created that feeling but now he realised it was probably something innate, stemming from her childhood. That was no surprise really. Her childhood had hardly been a stable, peaceful one.

While his own life had begun on rather shaky ground, he'd had the good fortune to have been given a solid, happy childhood. Annie's situation had been somewhat different and, he suspected, far more complicated. He didn't do complicated.

While Annie intrigued him, he didn't really want to become involved. Becoming involved meant giving up some control and that was something he preferred not to do so he'd tried his best to avoid her. But he'd only lasted a couple of days before he'd begun looking for excuses to see her. Searching for cases they had in common, reasons why he'd need to seek her out.

Kylie Jones had been his best option, although

not a very good one. Annie didn't need his input and, as she'd said, they didn't need to have lunch to discuss her situation. Anything Caspar had to say could have been said in a sentence or two as they passed in the corridor. He'd known that but it hadn't been enough for him. He'd wanted to see Annie.

He had tried to ignore the stirrings of desire that had been present ever since he'd watched her bending over to feed the cat, the Lycra of her exercise pants moulding to her bottom. He had tried to keep busy with work and filming the series and in any spare moments going with Brigitte to visit nursing homes, albeit without success at this stage.

He could still recall when the shoulder of Annie's sloppy joe had slipped to reveal her collarbone and the little hollow at the base of her throat, just the spot he always thought begged to be kissed, and ever since he'd had difficulty keeping thoughts of Annie Simpson out of his head.

He'd tried to tell himself that lust and desire were just chemistry, that physical attraction didn't necessarily make them compatible, but it was a difficult thing to ignore, particularly when he didn't really believe it.

Although he did suspect that, beyond their chemistry, they were unlikely to have much else in common. She wasn't his type. She was the type to feed other people's cats, the type who lived in a house that was too big for her and spent her spare time looking at paint charts and redecorating rooms as she made a home for herself. She wanted to settle down. He wasn't guessing. She'd said as much. She wanted a home and he suspected she'd want a family to go along with that home.

He lived in an apartment he didn't own and had never bothered decorating beyond new bed linen and matching towels. He hadn't lived in one place since he'd been thirteen, first boarding school for five years then university colleges, share houses and a couple of years overseas before returning to Melbourne. He had never missed having a place to call home and he'd never thought about putting down roots.

Annie was the type who would want happy

endings and romance. Hearing about her childhood convinced him that she would want the
fairy-tale ending and he couldn't blame her for
that. But he didn't believe in fairy-tales.

He'd be a fool to pursue her. She wasn't the
type of woman he could discard after a few dates.
He should stay away.

But chemistry was a hard thing for him to ignore and he was finding her irresistible.

He needed to find a reason for her to spend
more time with him. He needed to create an opportunity or a reason. But his mind was blank.
He decided to make small talk while he racked
his brain for a legitimate project. 'What did you
think of my big sister?' he asked.

'I liked her.'

Caspar laughed. 'You sound surprised,' he said.
'She didn't remind you of me, then?'

'Actually, she did. A little. I got the feeling she
could be as stubborn as you.'

'Is that good or bad?' He couldn't resist asking
the question.

'You don't want to know.' She smiled and he
felt as though the sun had come out. It was a ri-

diculous expression and not one he'd ever understood before, but now it made perfect sense. 'I thought her programme for teenage mothers was amazing. I'm really keen to work with her on that some more if I can.'

Unwittingly Annie had handed him a perfect idea. He could be the common link between them and maybe he could even find a way of featuring the project in the television series, which would give him a legitimate reason to be involved.

'What did you have in mind?' he asked.

'I'm not sure. It depends what's under way already. How did she become so involved in it? It seems above and beyond what I imagine is the job description of a school principal.'

'We were all brought up to have a social conscience and encouraged to support a cause. Brigitte's cause is teenage pregnancy.'

'And what is yours?' she asked, and Caspar gave himself a mental high five. She was interested enough to ask more. Surely that was a good sign?

'It's a long story. Why don't you meet me for a drink after work and I'll tell you then?' He felt marginally guilty about using her curiosity to his advantage but not guilty enough to stop.

Annie wasn't sure if she'd heard him correctly. Was he was asking her out for a drink for a second time?

'Don't you take no for an answer?'

'I don't often get knocked back.' He grinned and Annie knew he wasn't being arrogant, just honest.

She wished she'd met him under different circumstances. She was beginning to think she could really grow to like him, in a purely platonic sense, of course. She wasn't interested in anything else. Not any more. She sucked at relationships.

'I can't,' she told him.

'Can't or won't?'

'Won't,' she admitted. 'You do realise you've been here for two weeks and you've been on the front page of the local paper twice and on the evening news as well. I'm not interested in being fodder for the local gossip columnist, and even if it's an innocent drink I'm sure it won't be portrayed that way. I don't want to invite the media into my life.'

'Can't blame a man for trying,' he said. 'What about tomorrow night?' he asked, obviously unwilling to give up just yet. 'You are coming to the pub to watch the screening of the first episode of the series, aren't you? Can I buy you a drink then?'

The senior hospital staff and several of the nurses and admin personnel had received invitations earlier in the week to attend a function at the Royal Hotel to watch the first episode of *RPE at Blue Lake*. Annie was sure the television network was hosting the event. 'I thought the network was paying for it?'

'They are,' he admitted. 'I was just making sure you had accepted the invite. Brigitte is coming, you'll be able to chat to her about your ideas then. There will be a crowd of people but no cameras.'

She nodded as she stood and stacked her lunch tray. 'I'll be there.'

'Good, it's a date.'

She looked up from her tray and opened her mouth, ready to protest, but before she could say anything he winked at her and she realised she'd be making a fuss over what was essentially a throw-away line. He didn't mean anything by it.

But despite knowing it was a throw-away line and despite telling herself she wasn't interested in dating, she found herself racing home from work the following day and spending a ridiculous amount of time deliberating over what to wear to the pub.

In the end she figured that to wear anything unusual would invite questions so she stuck with a casual outfit of jeans and wedge heels. The only concession she made was to choose a camisole top in a pale yellow silk that she knew suited her colouring.

She was deliberately late, not late enough to miss the start of the show, just late enough to make sure she would have other people there to act as buffers between her and Caspar. Of course, it made no difference. He came across to her as soon as she arrived.

She watched him as he crossed the room, weaving through the crowd. He was wearing soft, faded jeans that moulded to his thighs and a black polo shirt. He had a casual, tossed-together look, as though five minutes ago he'd been naked and had just quickly thrown on the first clothes that had been to hand. Yet the result wasn't untidy, as she might have expected, but effortlessly sexy.

Her breathing quickened, keeping time with her heart as heat flooded through her belly. Caspar continued walking towards her. He was wickedly handsome, potently male and dangerously hot. He had a devilish gleam in his eye and Annie could imagine him holding out his hand in a silent invitation and she knew she would follow. She wouldn't be able to resist.

He held out his hand and smiled. 'Hello. I believe I owe you a drink,' he said, as he offered her a glass of champagne.

Her fantasy bubble burst but it was just as well. She was falling for something that wasn't even real, something that was a product of her hyperactive imagination. She focussed on reality. 'If I accept it, will you tell me about your story?'

'My story?'

'About your cause. You did promise.'

'And I am a man of my word.' He took a sip of his beer. 'Paediatrics is my cause.'

'Isn't that your career?' she protested. 'You can't fob me off with a made-up cause, otherwise I'll accuse you of getting me here under false pretences.'

He grinned and her stomach did a lazy somersault.

'I swear to tell the whole truth and nothing but the truth,' he said, as he made the sign of a cross over his heart. 'Medicine is my career but I chose paediatrics in particular. I guess, more correctly, I should say that children are my cause.'

'What does that mean exactly?'

'Remember I said it was a long story?' he said with a raised eyebrow. 'Are you sure you're ready for this?'

When Annie nodded he continued. 'Paediatrics was my favourite rotation but it all started long before that. It starts with my mother. She was born in Australia during World War Two to parents who were German immigrants. Because of their heritage they were classed as enemy aliens and interned in a camp for the duration of the war.'

'A camp in Australia?'

Annie was surprised when Caspar nodded. She'd had no idea that such things had existed in Australia.

'My mother was born in the camp,' Caspar continued. 'Her parents were Australian citizens but because they had been born in Germany they were detained against their wishes. My mother grew up being taught to speak up against injustice and she passed that on to us. She thought it was important that those of us who had a voice spoke up for those who didn't.

'Whenever we thought someone wasn't being given a fair hearing we were encouraged to actively do something about it. Brigitte has taken on pregnant teenagers, Krissy is a foster-mum and I studied medicine, and that led me to paediatrics.

'I want to protect children from harm. So many children don't have a voice either because they are too young or they are abused or disadvantaged or just ignored or unwanted. They need someone to listen to their story or ask questions on their be-half or fight for them. That's what I do.'

Annie had barely heard Caspar's last sentences. She hadn't heard much after 'foster-mum'. Those words always put her into a bit of a spin. She'd had first-hand experience with foster situa-tions and hadn't much cared for it. When Cas-par stopped speaking she quickly tried to think of something to say that wouldn't let him guess she hadn't been paying attention.

'Your mum must have been very proud of you,' she said.

'I'd like to think so but I also know she ex-pected nothing less from us. Sometimes I think our efforts are only a drop in the ocean but at least we're trying.'

'I think it's amazing that you're all so commit-ted. Is Brigitte here? I'd like to talk to her about her work.' Annie didn't want to spend too long talking to Caspar, she didn't want to monopolise his time. She was worried that people would no-tice and start to comment. Talking to Brigitte in-stead was a good alternative. But it wasn't to be.

'No. She can't make it. Dad's having a bad

day and Brig didn't want to leave him. He's not recognising her husband or kids today and she didn't want to leave him with people he thinks are strangers,' he explained. 'I've told her you are keen to be involved in her project and she'll call you. I hope that's okay.'

'Yes, that's fine,' Annie said, as she tried to think of another way to excuse herself, but she was saved by Tori's arrival. In Annie's mind, adding a third person to their conversation would attract less attention.

'Hi, what have I missed?' Tori asked. She was looking carefully from Annie to Caspar, but Annie wasn't about to divulge anything.

'Nothing,' she told her. 'We were just talking about work.' That wasn't quite true but Tori didn't have time to question her further as Gail commandeered a microphone to make a short speech before the show began.

Tori, Annie and Caspar were at the back of the room. 'Shouldn't you be up at the front?' Annie asked Caspar as the lights were dimmed and the opening credits rolled. She was all too aware of his proximity.

'No, I'm fine here,' he replied.

His voice was a whisper in her ear. It sent a tingle through her and she could feel her nipples harden. God, she was ridiculous. She needed to get a grip. She should move but there was nowhere to go without drawing more attention to herself. She tried to relax as the show began. Tried to ignore Caspar sitting beside her.

The show opened with an aerial scene shot from a helicopter as it flew across Blue Lake, before heading over the town and out to the farms, vineyards and pine plantations that surrounded the regional centre. The landscape was green and extremely picturesque but the voiceover was talking about the dangers lurking beneath the beauty.

The scene changed to a low-angle shot taken by the roadside, showing the huge logging trucks racing along the highways before the camera angle changed yet again, and now the audience could watch as the camera followed a truck. From the angle of the shot it was clear that it was being filmed from a car, a car that was dwarfed by the enormous tree trunks that were strapped to the trailer and towered above the car.

Annie knew exactly where Gail was heading with these pictures: the show was going to begin with Suzanne's accident. The husband suffering spinal injuries, the wife eighteen weeks pregnant, who had sustained terrible abdominal injuries. Annie held her breath, not sure she was ready to watch this on screen.

The screen went black but the audio continued. There were several seconds of metal shrieking, glass shattering and people screaming and then silence before the picture returned. The camera was now focussed on an ambulance parked in front of Blue Lake Hospital.

Annie kept watching—she didn't want to but she found herself unable to look away. She heard the paramedics telling her and Tang that Suzanne was pregnant. She could hear orders being yelled and could see people running to and fro.

She was only vaguely aware of her own role. There were so many people involved it was difficult to make out who was who, and she knew the audience would have an even harder time keeping track of all the people. No doubt they would be focussed on the drama rather than the doctors and nurses.

The voiceover was telling the audience that Suzanne was going for scans and the picture cut to a different patient, an orthopaedic case, before going to the birth of Kylie's twins, establishing the three cases that were obviously going to feature in the first episode.

Annie relaxed as the orthopaedic story was told. This case had nothing to do with her, and she remained relaxed as the show returned to Kylie Jones's segment, but her composure was short-lived. Liam had captured Kylie batting her eyelashes at Caspar but Annie hadn't expected him to include her as well. The scene in which she'd handed Caspar the first twin had been included and Annie was intensely aware that she was gazing at Caspar. She hoped no one else would notice but she could feel Tori watching her. The next ad break couldn't come soon enough.

After the ad break the show returned to Suzanne's case. The CT scan had been done and Suzanne was now in Theatre. The camera panned around the theatre, taking in the beeping machines, the bags of blood, the gowned and masked theatre staff, the scans on the light box and the patient on the table.

The camera focussed on Annie. She wasn't mentioned by name and she knew it would be difficult to recognise her underneath the cap and mask and shapeless gown, but she knew it was her. The scene showed her making an incision into Suzanne's abdomen. The camera was focussed on the wound. There was an awful lot of blood, which would make it difficult for the audience to see what was going on. Annie's hands were also in the shot, partially blocking the view, but she didn't need to watch to know what was happening. She knew what she'd found.

The shot cut away from Suzanne's abdomen and onto bloodied drapes. Annie squeezed her eyes closed, afraid to watch what came next.

She heard her own voice say, 'Oh, my God.' She couldn't believe this was happening. She couldn't believe they were going to show Suzanne's dead baby.

Annie opened her eyes and stood up. Other people might be willing to watch that, although they probably wouldn't have a choice as they wouldn't have any warning, but she couldn't sit there, knowing what was coming next. To her relief the show cut to another ad break, which gave her time to hurry from the room. She needed to get out of there.

Caspar had lied to her. He'd agreed that people wouldn't want to see this and yet it looked as though they were going to. Maybe Gail had persuaded him that it should be included, but if that was the case Annie was still disappointed in him. She paused in the passage while she thought about what she should do. She wasn't sure if she could go back into the room. She was relieved that the function room was upstairs and the hallway was empty as it gave her time to gather her thoughts. Or it would have except that Caspar had followed her out.

'Are you all right?' he asked.

'Of course not.' Annie put her hands on her hips as she prepared to give Caspar a piece of her mind. Not that he should need to hear her opinion, he should have a fair idea about what she had to say. 'I can't believe you're going to show that scene.'

'We're—'

'How could you?'

'I—'

'You can't tell me the audience will want to see that.'

'Will—?'

'It's far too confronting. Do you want people to change the channel? I can't believe I listened to you. I trusted you—'

Caspar took one step towards her, closing the small gap that separated them. In an instant his head dipped down and he pressed his lips to hers. The rest of her sentence disappeared into his kiss.

Caspar St Claire was kissing her!

Involuntarily, Annie closed her eyes as his mouth covered hers. His lips were warm and soft but his kiss was far from gentle. It was demanding and insistent and powerful and made her insides tremble. It was firm enough to take her breath away and make her swallow her words. His five-o'clock shadow was rough against her cheek but even that sensation was pleasant. She should protest, she should resist, but he wasn't giving her a chance and she didn't really want him to stop. For a moment she even thought about kissing him back.

CHAPTER SEVEN

THE KISS ENDED almost as quickly as it had begun. Within seconds her lips were free and she felt them spring back into shape as he lifted his mouth from hers.

She opened her eyes. She knew she should be angry. What exactly did he think he was doing? But the overwhelming emotion she felt was desire.

His kiss had been forceful and demanding and she'd felt it reverberate through her entire body, but he hadn't given her time to respond and she realised, as he freed her mouth, that she wanted to respond, she *would* have responded.

Perhaps it was just as well the kiss had been brief and unexpected, otherwise she might very well have made a fool of herself.

'What was that for?' she asked, once she'd recovered her equilibrium.

'You weren't giving me a chance to defend my-self. I had to shut you up so I could get a word in.'

'You could have asked,' she argued.

'Asked to kiss you? What would you have said?' He was smiling at her, enjoying himself.

She couldn't be angry. Moments before she'd been enjoying herself too.

'No, asked me to be quiet,' she clarified.

'I tried—'

'Well—'

Caspar reached out and put one finger on her lips. 'Are you going to let me speak now or do I need to kiss you again? Believe me, I'd be happy to.'

She blushed and folded her arms across her chest. 'Be my guest.'

He leant towards her and Annie realised he'd taken her words as an invitation to kiss her a sec-ond time. She put a hand out against his chest, stopping him from leaning any closer. As much as she would enjoy another chance, now was not the time or place. 'I *meant* have your say.'

'Oh.' He was grinning widely now, one eye-brow cocked in amusement, and it was enough to make Annie feel as though she could melt into a warm pool of desire at his feet.

'We don't show Suzanne's baby,' he told her. 'Gail wouldn't dream of it and if she had wanted to, I would have demanded that the scene be cut. I think losing a child is the worst thing in the world and, as I told you before, no one needs to see that. When the show comes back to Suzanne's story it cuts to a shot of me handing the baby to the nurse. He's wrapped, the audience don't see him, they see my back, and the theatre staff's tears and then Colin arrives to start the orthopaedic surgery. Come back and watch the rest. You'll see I'm telling you the truth.'

Annie shook her head. She couldn't go back into the room. Not because she didn't want to watch the show but because she couldn't return to the crowd after being kissed. She wanted to savour that for a little longer. She wanted to keep it to herself, she didn't want to be distracted by the show or her colleagues.

'No. I think I'll go home.'

He didn't try to kiss her again, neither did he try to persuade her to stay. He just looked at her carefully, before nodding his head and returning to the room.

Annie barely remembered the drive home. All she could think was that he'd kissed her and it had been every bit as lovely as she'd imagined it would be. But it couldn't happen again.

She wasn't ready for a relationship or any sort of tryst, for want of a better word. She had made a promise to herself that she would steer clear of any romantic involvement. She had a terrible track record and she had other things to focus on. And no matter how handsome Caspar St Claire was, or how well he kissed, he wasn't right for her.

But that wasn't enough to stop her from turning on the television when she got home. Aggie, the very pregnant cat, was waiting for her and she let her up beside her as she got comfortable on the couch and found the right channel. She told herself she wanted to see what unfolded in the rest of the programme and she was glad to see that when the show returned to Suzanne's story, Caspar had told her the truth. There was no footage of the baby. Instead, the camera panned to the faces of the staff, who were all in tears, and the outcome was self-explanatory.

But while Annie was glad Caspar had been honest, she knew her real motivation for watching the show was so she could watch him. The camera loved him. The strong contours of his face caught the light, casting shadows in just the right places, and his olive skin was a lovely foil for his dark hair and green eyes. His presence on screen drew one's attention. It was no wonder the viewers couldn't get enough of him.

She'd seen for herself the effect he'd had on her patients. And she imagined plenty of women would have liked to have been in her shoes just a short time ago. And then she wondered just how many had been in her shoes. She'd seen plenty of photos of him with different women on his arm and there were probably many more whose photos she hadn't seen.

Had he meant anything at all by the kiss? She was reliving it and getting herself all worked up about it while he'd probably meant it as nothing more than what he'd said it was, a way to shut her up. He'd probably already forgotten all about it. She should do the same.

'Where's Annie?' Tori asked Caspar when he returned to his seat.

'She went home,' he said, as he tried to ignore the empty chair between them. While Tori didn't know what had transpired, the vacant chair was a reminder to him of his spontaneous indiscretion.

Tori frowned. 'Is she okay?'

'She thinks we're going to show Suzanne's baby.' That was only part of the problem but it was all he was prepared to divulge to Tori and it was enough of a reason to explain Annie's absence. Tori had been the anaesthetist and would know what had happened next.

'I hope she's wrong.'

'Of course she is. I tried to tell her but she doesn't want to watch.'

'Okay.' Tori nodded. 'I'll call past her house later.'

'It's all right, I told her I would,' he fibbed, hoping Tori wouldn't argue with him. He knew he should let Tori check on Annie. He knew he should leave Annie alone. But he couldn't do it. Someone needed to make sure she was okay and he'd rather it was him.

The programme ended on a happier note with footage of Kylie and Paul in the nursery holding their twins. He wondered if Annie was watching.

The minute he thought he could escape without anyone noticing, he headed for his car. Annie had tasted as good as he'd expected. Her lips had been warm and forgiving under his and she hadn't resisted, even though she must have been taken by surprise. He had surprised himself.

He didn't stop to consider if Annie would mind him calling at her home. He couldn't think straight after that kiss—all he could think about was getting a chance to do it again.

He knocked on her kitchen door. The scent of jasmine engulfed him as he waited, evoking memories of her, but he knew the smell came from the plant that clung to the back veranda. The creeper was heavy with flowers, their perfume thick in the warm, still night air. He knocked a second time and the door opened.

The pregnant cat was winding herself around

Annie's ankles, drawing Caspar's attention to her legs. She had changed out of her jeans into soft shorts that displayed her sensational legs to full effect. She was barefoot now and from his height advantage he could see the swell of her cleavage under her shirt. On the drive between the pub and Annie's house he had thought about what he wanted to say but the moment he saw her standing in the doorway all he could think of was how she tasted.

He wanted to kiss her again but not without an invitation this time. One spontaneous kiss was possibly all he would be able to get away with.

'What are you doing here?'

He could hardly class that sentence as an invitation.

'I wanted to know if you saw the end of the show,' he said. 'Whether you've forgiven me.'

'Forgiven you?' she asked. 'I saw the end. You were right about the footage. I should be asking you to forgive me for jumping to conclusions.'

'I was talking about forgiving me for kissing you.'

'Oh.'

'I shouldn't have done that,' he said, as his gaze drifted to her soft, pink lips. 'But…' His words drifted off into silence as he let himself be distracted by her mouth.

'But what?' Annie's voice was whisper quiet.

'But, so help me, I'd like to do it again.'

She didn't say anything in reply. She just stood there looking up at him with her enormous brown eyes and pouty pink lips, and it was all Caspar could do not to scoop her up in his arms and carry her into the house.

And then she stepped back, out of the doorway, making room for him to move inside. That was all the invitation he needed.

He stepped into the kitchen and kicked the door closed behind him.

The door slammed shut. Caspar was in her kitchen, inches from her.

She shouldn't have let him in but she had been powerless to resist. Her body continued to betray her, operating independently of her mind. She could feel herself being drawn to him. Her breaths were shallow and she could feel her nipples harden as he looked at her with his green eyes almost daring her to close the gap between them.

She never knew if she reached for him or if he reached for her, but in an instant she was in his arms with her hands wound behind his neck.

He bent his head.

She lifted her face and his lips met hers. They were warm and soft but the pressure was firm. He was taking control, taking what he wanted, and she was letting him. She wanted it too and this time there was no reason to stop.

His tongue teased her lips and she parted them in response to his pressure. She tasted him, minty, sweet and warm.

She wanted him, badly, inexplicably. She'd never felt like this before. She had an overwhelming, overpowering need to taste and touch and hold another person and to have them hold her.

For the first time she thought maybe she could understand why her mother had been unable to resist her father. If their chemistry was anything like this, it would be almost impossible to resist.

But she had to resist, she had to be stronger than her mother had been.

She took her hands from behind his head, removing her fingers from the dark curls at the nape of his neck and dropping her arms to her sides. She stepped back. She was breathing loudly, panting, her breaths coming in short, shallow bursts. She needed to tell him to stop but she couldn't speak.

'Which way is your bedroom?' It seemed he still had the power of speech.

She should stop him now. But she couldn't.

'Front of the house, on the right.' Somehow she found the strength to answer.

Before she'd even finished the sentence Caspar had picked her up and was carrying her down the hall. Her reply had obviously been taken as consent. A fair assumption, she supposed. She could have said no. But that was unlikely to happen. She didn't have the willpower to resist.

She didn't bother to protest. She didn't want to. She wanted this. Maybe more than she'd wanted anything ever before.

Her legs were wrapped around his waist, his

hands, warm and large, cupped her buttocks, holding her close. The heat of his palms seared through the thin fabric of her shorts. He dropped little kisses on her mouth and throat as he carried her the short distance down the hall. He paused in the doorway of her room, Annie nodded her head and he stepped inside, and for the second time that night he kicked a door closed with his foot.

Annie lay on her back, her head turned to the side as she watched Caspar propped on one elbow, watching her. She didn't have the words to describe how she was feeling, which was just as well as she didn't have the energy to speak. She didn't have the energy to move.

They were both naked, the bed sheet covering them from the waist down leaving Annie's breasts exposed. Caspar reached out and brushed her breast with his fingertips and her nipple peaked instantly, her body responding instinctively and involuntarily to his touch, ready for more.

Until tonight she'd only ever slept with one man, her husband, and in the beginning sex had been interesting, enjoyable even, but it had never been like this. It had never been the all-consuming, passionate, amazing experience that she'd read about. Until now.

She couldn't believe she was twenty-nine years old and was only just finding out what she'd been missing all these years. Her resolution to stay away from men was looking a little flimsy. Sex like that would be enough to make her change her mind about a lot of things. She didn't think she was strong enough to resist. Perhaps she was more like her mother than she wanted to be.

She was glad they hadn't taken it slowly. Glad she hadn't had time to think about what she was doing. She might have found the willpower to stop and then she would have missed out on the best sex she'd ever had.

'Are you okay?' Caspar asked, before he bent his head and covered her breast with his mouth. He flicked his tongue over her erect nipple, making her moan with pleasure. He lifted his head and replaced his tongue with his fingers. He was smiling at her. 'You're very quiet. Have I just discovered the secret to stop you from arguing with me?'

Annie laughed as she arched her back towards him, pushing her breast further into his hand as if she was afraid he might stop. She couldn't believe how good she felt. 'I just realised what all the fuss is about,' she said.

'So no regrets?'

'Not regrets as such.'

'But…?'

'I didn't mean to get myself in this situation. I moved down here to have a fresh start. Not to jump into bed with the first man who crosses my doorstep.'

'Really? I'm the first man to be in your house?' He sounded pleased and a little surprised.

'Not exactly, but Bert, my landlord, is an octogenarian. I think he's safe from any advances on my part but I certainly wasn't planning on having sex with you.'

'Why not?'

'Oh. Let's see.' Annie fought hard to concentrate but it was extremely difficult while Caspar continued to tease her nipple with his tongue.

'I barely know you,' she said, as he moved his mouth to her other breast. 'We work together,' she moaned, as he ran his tongue from her breast to her belly button. 'This is completely out of character for me and I've only been divorced for six months.'

That was enough to break his concentration. He lifted his head. 'You were married?'

'Yes.' Annie gave a half-smile. It would almost be funny if it wasn't true. But on this occasion she was pleased she was divorced as if she were still married she would have missed out on tonight. On him. 'The last man I slept with had to marry me first.'

He grinned at her. 'I didn't realise a precedent had been set. I wasn't planning on proposing.'

'That's good, because I never want to get married again. I just meant I don't usually sleep with strangers.'

'I'm not a stranger,' he said, as he slid his hand under the sheet and between her thighs. Annie's knees fell apart, proving his point.

'Maybe you're not a total stranger,' she admitted, 'but you don't really know anything about me.'

'I know you smell like jasmine and you moan in a very sexy way when you orgasm.'

Annie felt herself blush. 'That doesn't count.'

'All right, then. Tell me something you think I should know.'

Annie struggled to think of something while Caspar's fingers were busy under the sheet, distracting her. 'I've never had a one-night stand,' she said.

'And I vote we keep it that way. I'm more than happy to repeat tonight's events,' he replied, before pausing slightly. He was frowning. 'Have you slept with *anyone* since your divorce?'

Annie wondered if she should tell him she hadn't slept with anyone since long *before* her divorce. She couldn't actually remember the last time she'd had sex. She hadn't really missed it. Now she wondered how she'd ever survive without it.

She shook her head.

Caspar removed his hand from between her thighs and slid it around her hips to cup her bottom. He pulled her towards him and she could feel his erection pressing against her stomach, but he seemed unaware of it. He was focussing on her. 'If I'd known, I would have done things differently. Taken it slowly.'

'It's fine. Better than fine. It was just what I needed.'

Caspar doubted that. Annie should have had some romance. She was right. They were virtually strangers. He should have spent more time getting to know her. Not knowing a person was fine if it was only a one-time thing but he didn't want this to be a one-night stand. She deserved better.

'Do you think we could start again tomorrow?' he asked as he nuzzled her neck. 'I'll take you to dinner first, do things properly. We could even try having a conversation first.'

But Annie shook her head.

'Okay, we'll skip the conversation but you have to eat,' he teased, and to his relief she laughed.

'I don't mind the conversation but I don't really want to go out to eat. I don't want to draw attention to myself or invite questions, and I think that's unavoidable if I'm with you. You're a celebrity around here.'

'Only a minor one,' he retorted.

'Enough to make it impossible to have a quiet dinner, I'd imagine.'

'Why don't I pick up some dinner and bring it here, then? Would that be okay?'

He wanted a chance to make it something more than a frenzied, albeit passionate and thoroughly enjoyable experience. He wanted to make it special. He knew what to do. She just had to agree.

Annie nodded and he felt a surge of satisfaction. He'd been worried she would find more excuses.

Annie dragged herself to the gym the following day. She ached in strange places. Muscles she'd forgotten she had complained every time she moved but the ache wasn't unpleasant. Tori was waiting for her and Annie tried to be enthusiastic, even though she didn't want to be there.

She wanted to be back in her bed with Caspar. Her legs were only just strong enough to hold her up and she hadn't quite recovered her focus or strength after last night. Her mind kept wandering and her body kept threatening to collapse with exhaustion.

'Were you okay last night?' Tori asked. 'You left early.'

Annie could scarcely believe so much had happened in the past twelve hours. So much had changed.

'Did Caspar call at your place?' Tori added, when Annie didn't reply.

'Mmm-hmm.'

'So what happened?'

'What do you mean?'

'Did he stay for a drink? Did you let him take you to bed for that steamy sex I've been waiting to hear about?'

'What?' Annie immediately wanted to run and hide. What had made Tori ask that question? Had Caspar said something?

'There was enough heat between you both to fry an egg,' Tori said. 'I thought, hoped, you might get carried away.'

Annie breathed a sigh of relief. Tori was only fishing for information but her description was enough to make Annie blush, despite the sense of relief. She could feel heat suffusing her cheeks and cursed her tendency to turn scarlet. Of course Tori noticed.

'You did, didn't you? Well done,' she cheered. 'Was it fantastic?'

Annie opened and closed her mouth without divulging anything. She had no idea how to respond to that question.

Tori held up a hand. 'No, that's okay. You don't need to tell me, but are you seeing him again?'

'He's coming over tonight,' Annie admitted, knowing Tori would get that information out of her eventually anyway. 'But I don't know what to do.'

'What do you mean? You sleep with him again. It's not a difficult decision.'

'It is, considering I've only ever slept with one other man.'

Tori's eyebrows almost disappeared into her hairline. 'You're kidding.'

Annie shook her head. 'I wish I was.'

'Well, in that case I suggest that you don't think about it, don't analyse it. Just use him for sex.'

Tori laughed. 'He can be your post-divorce gift to yourself.'

'That doesn't seem like much of a relationship,' Annie said.

'But you don't want a relationship, do you?' Tori argued. 'He's only here for a few weeks. Why don't you have some fun? You can have mind-blowing sex without the relationship. In fact, in your current situation I'd recommend it. But it's your choice.'

Annie's body was still humming with a post-coital glow and she knew she didn't *have* a choice. She couldn't give him up. Not yet.

Annie heard Caspar's car pull to a stop out the front of her house. She'd been listening for the sound of his Audi for the past thirty minutes. She had planned on being cool, calm and collected but her body seemed to have a different idea and she found herself waiting at the back door to let him in.

He was wearing his soft jeans again and a casual green and white striped cotton shirt. He had the sleeves rolled up to his elbows and in his arms he held a box filled with containers of Indian takeaway. She could smell cumin, coriander and jasmine rice.

He put the box down on the kitchen table and Annie could see that in his hand he held a bunch of flowers. 'For you,' he said as he handed them to her. It was a colourful assortment of sweet peas and she had the perfect vase. An old ceramic milk jug sat on the mantelpiece above the stove. She pulled it down and filled it with water, pleased to have something to keep her busy. Pleased to have something to stop her from throwing herself straight into his arms.

A little bit of control wouldn't go astray, she thought, if only she could summon some. As part of her intended cool, calm and collected approach she had planned on trying to eat first but now all she could think of was ripping Caspar's clothes off—starting with unbuttoning his shirt.

The mental image of sliding his shirt from his shoulders to reveal his broad chest underneath distracted her from the task at hand and by the time she had eventually arranged the flowers he had pulled several take-away containers from the box. The containers were stacked in two piles and there was enough food to feed four.

Annie frowned. 'Are we expecting more people?' She hadn't intended on sharing him.

'Making love builds an appetite,' he said as he winked at her, and Annie was tempted to start getting rid of his shirt right then and there, but she forced herself to slow things down as much as she was capable of doing.

She smiled as she lifted the lid on one container to peek inside. 'You're getting a little ahead of yourself, don't you think? I thought we'd eat first.'

'Well, that's disappointing,' he replied, as he reached out and ran a finger down her bare arm. A surge of desire shot through her and it was so powerful she nearly gave in on the spot.

She looked at the foil containers stacked on the table and then she looked at Caspar. 'Maybe we could put the containers into the oven,' she suggested.

'Now, there's a good idea.' He grinned and Annie's insides wobbled.

He picked up the containers and slid them into

the oven. Annie followed him across the kitchen and bent over to turn the oven on. Caspar was behind her now and she felt him push her hair off her neck and then his lips were on her skin, kissing the back of her neck where it sloped down to her shoulder, setting her nerves on fire.

Her dress zipped at the back and as she straightened up, his fingers slid the zip down, exposing her spine. His hand was inside her dress and his fingers skimmed her waist as he slid his hand around over her rib cage and cupped her breast. Annie moaned with longing as his fingers brushed her nipple.

'You're not playing fair,' she said, as she turned round to face him.

'You'll have to teach me the rules then,' he said before his head dipped down and he claimed her mouth with his.

Annie closed her eyes as she kissed him back while she let her fingers work blindly, furiously, to undo the buttons on his shirt. She slid it from his shoulders and ran her hands down his chest, over the ridge of his abdominals and lower still until she could feel his erection under her palm, and it was his turn to moan.

He shrugged his hands out of his sleeves and dropped his shirt on the kitchen floor as they left a trail of clothes strewn behind them on their way to her bedroom.

CHAPTER EIGHT

FOR THE SECOND time in as many nights they lay, naked and spent, beneath her sheets.

'I don't seem to be doing this right,' Caspar said.

Annie couldn't see how it could get any better but she wasn't brave enough to say so, scared she would highlight her own naivety. 'You don't hear me complaining,' she said.

'No, but I believe I promised you dinner and conversation.'

She sighed and rolled onto her side, facing him, pulling the sheet up and tucking it under her arm. He was smiling, his green eyes dark and gleaming.

'I don't have the energy to get up.' She couldn't be bothered moving.

'Shall we eat in here? I'll bring you something,' he offered. 'What do you fancy?'

You. But she was too shy to say it. 'You choose.'

He dropped a kiss on her bare shoulder before he swung his legs out of bed. He stood stark naked without a hint of timidity while Annie lay in bed and admired his butt as he walked from the room. She wished she had his self-confidence. When he touched her there was no room in her head for anything other than desire, but now that he was gone from her sight she worried that he might not return. What if he just kept on walking?

Now that their sexual appetite had been sated, all her self-doubt crept back again. What did he see in her? Why would he want her? What would he want *from* her?

To her relief, he returned. He'd found his underwear somewhere between her bedroom and the kitchen so he was no longer completely naked, which was a pity, she thought. His shirt was hanging over his arm and in that hand he held he held two wine glasses and a bottle of sauvignon blanc. Along the other arm he held two bowls, heaped with steaming food. She was impressed with his multi-tasking.

'Something smells good.'

'I aim to please,' he said, as he laid the wine and glasses on the bed, along with the bowls, before passing her his shirt. 'I thought you might want to wear this. The food is still hot and I'd hate you to spill something and burn yourself.'

Annie took his shirt, breathing deeply as she slid her arms into the sleeves. The shirt smelt of him. She did up a couple of buttons, just enough to preserve her modesty, as he poured her a glass of wine.

'Here's to us,' he said, as he raised his glass in a toast.

'Us?'

'Yes. A new beginning. Didn't we agree to start over again tonight?'

'I'm not sure we agreed exactly. I'm not sure about anything, I'm completely out of my depth,' she admitted. 'This is all new territory for me.'

'What is?'

She waved one hand vaguely in his direction, not quite sure how to phrase her feelings. Surely she couldn't tell him how inexperienced she was, how he had opened her eyes to sex? It might frighten him away and while she still wasn't sure exactly what she wanted, she was pretty sure it wasn't that.

'All of this. I've only ever had one physical relationship and that was with my husband.'

Caspar almost choked on his wine. 'How long were you married?

'Seven years.'

'And you've been divorced, what, six months?' She could see him trying to do the calculations. 'How old were you when you got married?'

'Twenty-one.'

'Why so young?' He was frowning as though she'd done something quite incomprehensible.

Annie supposed that amongst medical students getting married early was unusual but in the general population it wasn't that strange. Annie had spent many hours in the latter stages of her marriage analysing what had convinced her that marrying young was a good idea. She understood why she'd done it but she wasn't certain it would make sense to anyone else.

'My gran died when I was twenty. After my parents' death she was all I had and when she died she left a gaping hole in my life. Most people marry for love. Or money. I told myself I was in love but I wasn't. I was scared of being alone. I married for companionship.'

'What about him?'

'If I had to pick one of my two options I'd say "money" but I didn't realise it at the time. I thought we both wanted the same thing, needed the same thing, but my marriage cost me everything I had left.'

'Everything?'

She nodded. 'My home, my privacy, my job offer in Adelaide.' *My confidence too,* she thought.

'You moved down here to start again?'

'Yes. And I intend to do just that. I'm not going to make the same mistakes again. I have no intention of having a relationship with anyone, of getting involved.'

'By the look of us, I'd say we're already involved.'

'Yes, but I'm not sure how involved we should be.'

'What does that mean?'

'I'm no good at relationships. I'm complicated.'

'I already figured out the complicated part but I think it's time you had some fun.'

There was that word again. Fun. First Tori and now Caspar. But Annie wasn't sure she knew how to have fun, although, if it meant repeating last night, she reckoned she could be persuaded.

'I know you said you wanted to avoid the spotlight but we could keep it low-key. Private. Just like this,' he said.

'And what is this like exactly—a clandestine affair?' she asked.

'You've got to admit it's not a bad idea. There's no downside. We can have sex as much as we like and no one has to know.' He was smiling again, his green eyes had lightened in colour and she could see the brown flecks again. 'You can avoid attention and I don't have to share you.'

As an idea it did have some merit. She could have her cake and eat it too. But Annie wasn't going to be like her mother. She wasn't prepared to schedule her time around a man and needed to be able to keep the few commitments she had. Caspar would have to fit in with her too.

'I guess if we can find time that suits us both it could work,' she said, trying to play it low-key. 'And we have to keep things professional at work.'

Caspar agreed without argument and Annie was left wondering if she'd just made a terrible mistake. Caspar St Claire was well and truly out of the box and she hoped she wasn't going to regret it.

Annie wanted to keep their relationship discreet but it was impossible to avoid him at work, especially as Caspar seemed to find ways of being where she was. When Annie needed to speak to Suzanne about her future and whether she would be able to have more children, the film crew asked if they could film this meeting and Caspar, in his role as paediatrician, was there too. When it was time to film Kylie and Paul taking their twins home from the hospital they asked Annie to see them off and again Caspar was there.

No matter where Annie turned, Caspar materialised and that made her nervous. She was worried she wouldn't be able to hide her thoughts and reactions to him and that their relationship would become obvious to everyone, but Caspar, to his credit, played the game perfectly.

He didn't avoid physical contact but somehow he managed to disguise any contact at work, but her nerves made her abrupt and she looked forward to the evenings when they could be alone and she could relax and stop worrying about trying to keep their relationship a secret.

Tori, who had been sworn to secrecy over the affair, assured her that no one would guess there was anything going on and Annie found that, despite her reservations, a pattern very quickly emerged where they would spend several nights a week together. Annie insisted on continuing with her normal schedule, which included her gym classes with Tori, and on those nights Caspar would have dinner at Brigitte's and then come to her house.

On other nights they ate together but always at Annie's. Caspar continued to educate and excite Annie in the bedroom but she always made him leave before morning. She wasn't ready to let him stay the whole night.

At least once a week Caspar would be invited to a function, often a charity event, sometimes a social event, sometimes as a celebrity guest, sometimes as a guest speaker, and he always invited Annie to accompany him and she always refused. Tori badgered her about going but Annie couldn't bring herself to take the relationship public. She still had reservations, she still wasn't sure exactly what they were doing.

But Caspar was not so secretive. He wasn't used to sneaking around and, while he respected Annie's wish to avoid the media, after a couple of weeks he began to feel as though he was now leading a double or even triple life.

His work life had been split into two and now his personal life was going the same way. He had his normal work persona, his on-camera work persona and his private life, which was now divided into more pieces than he was used to—the life he shared with his family, the part he shared in public and then a third part he shared with Annie. He didn't know how long he could keep juggling all the different parts but he couldn't work out which one he could give up.

Cutting Annie from his life was really the only possibility, but he wasn't prepared to do that. Being in this situation was a novelty for him. He had never been the one to want more out of a relationship before and he wasn't sure if he liked the feeling. He wasn't sure if it equated to losing control but he wasn't ready to give her up. He enjoyed spending time with her and he wasn't prepared to deny himself that.

Instead, he tried to combine Annie with his social life, inviting her to several of the various and varied functions he found himself invited to, but she wasn't at all interested.

But one night when Annie was waylaid at the hospital with a delivery and had to cancel their plans, a different opportunity presented itself and Caspar grabbed it. In what he hoped she would take as a magnanimous gesture he met her at her house with leftovers from his dinner at Brigitte's. His sister was an excellent cook and he didn't think Annie would be able to refuse Brigitte's schnitzels with herbed potatoes. But Annie was more concerned about their privacy.

'She knows about us?'

'She won't say anything,' Caspar argued, before he played his trump card. 'I figured it's only fair that I could tell one person since you've told Tori.'

'You know about that?'

He nodded. 'I don't have a problem with people knowing about our relationship. You obviously trust Tori. I trust Brigitte and she's instructed me to invite you to dinner tomorrow night—she says it will give the two of you a chance to talk more about her teenage mothers project.' He appealed to her sense of duty, knowing she would then feel slightly obligated. He knew he was being sneaky but if it worked to his advantage he wasn't going to feel guilty. 'I'll be there too,' he added.

Annie nodded slowly, clearly thinking through the prospect before agreeing. 'Okay.'

She may be hesitant but at least she had agreed. He thought it would be nice to have somewhere non-threatening where they could meet, rather than always being cooped up in Annie's house. He would really like to take her away for a weekend, he wanted to wake up with her in the bed beside him, but to date she hadn't let him stay overnight and this secretive behaviour was beginning to wear thin. He was starting to feel as though she was ashamed of their relationship and he didn't like that feeling.

When Annie arrived at Brigitte's house she was pleased to see Caspar's car already parked outside, she felt better knowing Caspar would be there to break the ice. Annie and Brigitte had met once to discuss the project but that had been in Annie's office, a completely different environment from tonight's meeting, and Annie had to admit she would feel far more comfortable if their meetings were held in a more formal setting.

She was okay with meeting new people, she'd had plenty of experience, but she wasn't great at making friends. She'd learnt not to do that as eventually it would lead to learning about each other's lives, which always made her uneasy. Colleagues and patients were different, she wasn't expected to be sociable, but this was Caspar's family, and she realised, with some surprise, she wanted them to like her.

Caspar met her at the front door. He kissed her, which made her forget her nerves, took her hand and led her to the kitchen. To Annie's relief Brigitte was as relaxed and friendly as she'd been the last time they'd met, and her husband, Tom, was just as nice.

'Where's Dad?' Caspar asked Brigitte, as Tom poured everyone a glass of wine.

'He had an early dinner and has taken himself off to bed,' Brigitte replied. 'He's very tired at the end of the day, probably a result of his night-time wanderings. The number of times I get up during the night, it's like having a newborn again.'

'No news on an aged care bed for him yet?' Annie asked. She'd been curious to meet Caspar's father but it was probably better she didn't. It might just confuse him and there was really no need to meet him as she wasn't going to be a permanent part of Caspar's life.

Brigitte shook her head. 'No. I found out today that he is top of the list for the next available male bed at our preferred home, but who knows when that will be? I feel bad wishing it would happen soon 'cos that means another family will have lost someone in order for the bed to be vacated.'

'It's never easy, is it?' Annie agreed. She could imagine how difficult the whole situation must be. She'd been fortunate that her grandmother had been able to stay in her own home. Families came with a lot of additional worries and while she wished her life had been different, she wasn't sure the alternatives were necessarily always easier.

She was just about to offer to help Brigitte in the kitchen when they were interrupted by a new arrival. A heavily pregnant woman with fine, dead-straight, strawberry-blonde hair appeared in the family room.

Caspar went to greet her. 'Krissy, good to see you.' He kissed her on the cheek before turning to introduce her to Annie. 'Annie, this is my other sister, Kristin Scott.'

'We've met,' the woman said to Caspar as she extended her hand to Annie. 'Hello, Dr Simpson.'

Annie was confused. The woman was obviously pregnant, and Annie assumed she was a patient but she didn't recognise her straight away.

She racked her brain. Kristin Scott, it wasn't ringing any bells. It was also hard to believe she was Caspar's other sister. She looked nothing like either Caspar or Brigitte.

'You've met?' Caspar asked.

'Hello?' Kristin laughed and waved a hand over her swollen belly. 'I'm a pregnant woman, how many obstetricians do you think there are around here?'

So it seemed they had met at an antenatal visit. 'I haven't seen you for a while,' Annie said, hoping her assumption was correct. 'How many weeks are you now?'

'Thirty-seven,' Kristin replied. 'I saw one of the midwives last week.'

Kristin's wrists and arms were thin but her face was quite puffy and she looked tired and strained. That wasn't unusual at this stage of pregnancy, especially if she had other children at home, which Annie thought Caspar had said she did, but there was something about her that set alarm bells ringing for Annie.

She quickly swept her gaze over Kristin as she'd been trained to do. Kristin's calves and ankles seemed swollen and quite disproportionate to her upper limbs. She appeared to be retaining a lot of fluid.

'How are you feeling? Are things going well?' Annie questioned her carefully, not wanting to panic her if she was feeling good, but something made her doubt that.

'I've been fine, until today. That's why I called in. I came into town to do my grocery shopping but I'm really not feeling up to it. I have a splitting headache and I wondered, Brig,' she said, as she turned to her sister, 'if I could borrow Nikki or Sam? I could use their help with carrying the bags.'

Brigitte glanced from Kristin to Annie, a question in her eyes. She'd obviously picked up some of the subtle signs too. Annie shook her head, very slightly, enough to give Brigitte the answer she was looking for.

'Why don't you give me your list?' Brigitte replied. 'The kids can go and do your shopping for you. You look like you'd be better off putting your feet up for a bit.'

'I think that's a good idea,' Annie added. 'I

have my medical bag in my car. If you like, I can check your blood pressure.'

Kristin didn't argue, lending weight to Annie's initial theory that she was feeling far from well. Annie fetched her bag. As she'd expected, Kristin's blood pressure was high, and she also noted pitting oedema in her lower calves. 'I think we should take you into the hospital and do a urine test,' she told Kristin.

'Why?'

'Your BP is high, your ankles are swollen more than I think is acceptable and you're not feeling well. I need to check for pre-eclampsia. Do you have any family history of it?' Annie couldn't remember what they'd discussed in her initial antenatal visit.

'I didn't have any problems with my other two pregnancies,' Kristin replied. 'I can't tell you about any family history.'

That made no sense to Annie. Why wouldn't she have any details on her family history? Kristin didn't sound confused but perhaps her headache was interfering with her concentration.

Annie glanced at Brigitte, hoping she could fill her in.

'Kristin is our foster-sister,' Brigitte explained. 'She doesn't have any details about her birth mother's medical history.'

Annie tried to keep the surprise from showing on her face but she knew it would be evident to anyone who was watching her. Any time fostering was mentioned Annie knew it always came as a shock to her.

'Right.' She struggled to keep her tone neutral. 'Then I think it's best that we check this properly. In hospital. Are you happy for me to drive you?'

Kristin nodded while Brigitte began organising everyone. 'Caspar, why don't you go with Annie? That way you can call me from the hospital when you know what's happening. I'll send the kids to the supermarket to do the shopping and if necessary I'll drive out to Kristin's place and look after the kids so John can come into town.'

Brigitte seemed perfectly in tune with the role of eldest sibling and everyone else fell into line, including Caspar. Annie briefly wondered if she was the only one who seemed to butt heads with him, although she had to admit their arguments had decreased in intensity of late—they had been too busy expending their energy in other ways.

Within minutes Annie and Caspar had Kristin in the car and were en route to the hospital.

'Aren't you going to ring your camera crew?' Annie couldn't resist asking.

'No,' he replied.

'Why not? Is it because it involves your family?' she asked.

'No. I just don't think this is exciting enough for the programme. There's no real emergency, no drama. If the crew were already at the hospital I might think about it but I know they're not. I won't call them in for something that more than likely would get cut.'

Annie couldn't argue. She'd been prepared to be annoyed if he was avoiding filming because it was personal but she knew in this case he was probably right. Even if tests showed that Kristin did have pre-eclampsia, she was unlikely to require emergency intervention tonight.

Annie was quiet, lost in her own thoughts, for the remainder of the short drive.

When they arrived at the hospital Annie took Kristin straight into the emergency department, explaining it was quicker than admitting her. They could do that later if necessary.

'You'll need to give a urine sample,' she told her as she left her with Tang, the RMO on duty.

'That's one thing I have no problem with,' Kristin said.

When Annie returned, Kristin's BP was still high and the protein reading in her urine was more than she liked. 'You said you came into town to do your grocery shopping. Do you live far away?' she asked.

'We're on a vineyard, about thirty minutes away.'

'In that case, I'm going to admit you overnight,' Annie told her. 'I want to do a twenty-four-hour urine analysis and it's a lot easier to do it in hospital. I'm pretty sure you have pre-eclampsia but I want to do more investigations. Can your husband manage with the kids?'

'Of course. Caspar, can you ring John and tell him what's going on?' Kristin asked, and Caspar pulled out his mobile phone and left the room.

'I've heard of pre-eclampsia but I've never paid much attention. What is it exactly?'

'It's due to constriction of your blood vessels, which can cause high blood pressure and the swelling in your tissues, you can see that in your ankles, and it can cause your kidneys to leak protein,' Annie explained. 'It's normal to see some protein in your urine but your first reading was higher than I'd like.'

'Is it harmful to the baby?'

Annie knew that pre-eclampsia could lead to seizures or restriction of blood flow to the uterus or, in serious cases, organ failure, but considering she hadn't officially diagnosed the condition yet she didn't want to mention the worst-case scenarios. She informed Kristen that they would keep her in hospital for close monitoring and discuss other problems if and when it became necessary.

'How do you treat it?'

'For now, bed rest and monitoring. Bed rest is just to try to lower your blood pressure and we'll do the twenty-four-hour urine test and I'll order some blood tests as well. *Then*, if we confirm pre-eclampsia, the only cure is to deliver your baby. Once we deliver the placenta the condition will resolve. Your baby is old enough to be induced if necessary but, remember, everything may settle spontaneously.' Annie doubted that but it was better to leave Kristin feeling calm.

'I'll organise an ultrasound tomorrow to check your baby's development if I need to. For now, we'll take some blood and then admit you and transfer you to Maternity. You just have to try and rest in between going to the toilet and having your obs checked constantly.' She smiled, knowing how little rest Kristin would probably get.

'Easier said than done,' Kristin replied, 'but at least I won't have to get up to two other kids during the night.'

Annie admitted Kristin while she waited for Caspar and once Kristin had been transferred to Maternity it was just the two of them again.

'Is she going to be okay?' Caspar wanted to know.

Annie nodded.

'She must be feeling pretty crook, considering she didn't give any of us the third degree about why you were at Brigitte's. I initially thought she'd dropped in on purpose to check you out.'

'She knows about us too?'

'I didn't tell her but don't be surprised if Brigitte has. They're thick as thieves, those two.'

Terrific, Annie thought as she unlocked her car and wondered just how many other people were going to hear about their relationship through the grape vine.

'Shall we see if Brigitte has saved us some dinner?' Caspar suggested as they turned into her street.

'It's too late now, isn't it?'

'Brigitte will be up, she'll want to know how Kristin is.'

Annie didn't want to stay, she had too many questions competing for space in her head and not enough answers. 'Do you mind if I don't come in?' she said as she parked outside. 'I'll go home and get some rest in case I get a call about Kristin.'

'You don't want company?'

Annie shook her head.

'Are you okay? You've been quiet. I always worry when you're quiet.'

Annie knew that she was still feeling a bit thrown since hearing that Kristin had been a foster-child. It always made her cast her mind back and while she'd managed to concentrate on Kristin's needs while they had been at the hospital, now that her attention wasn't needed elsewhere she found herself distracted. She thought of a believable excuse. 'I don't want to intrude. I'm not used to family dynamics any more,' she said.

'Is that what's bothering you, my family?' he asked. 'I know we can be a bit overwhelming but it's not always that bad.' He smiled at her, his green eyes shining. 'We don't always have such major crises, at least not at dinnertime.'

'Your family is lovely. Kristin is very lucky…'

'We all are. Our lives would be very different if Mum and Dad hadn't made us a family.'

'What do you mean?'

'We're not biological siblings. Brig and I are adopted and Krissy is our foster-sister. Mum and Dad created our family in an unorthodox way, I suppose, but it was Mum's way of making a difference. Her way of taking care of those who didn't have a voice. We had lots of foster-kids living with us over the years but Kristin was the one who never left. She's just another sister to us, even though she wasn't adopted.'

'Why wasn't she?'

'Her mother refused to give her up, even though she wasn't interested in caring for her.'

'She was lucky to get your family. Not every child is so fortunate.' Annie was pensive as their conversation returned to the heart of the problem.

Caspar was frowning. 'You sound as though you know what you're talking about.' Annie realised he'd become very adept at reading her moods. Perhaps it was a legacy of growing up with two sisters, but Annie had learned that not much escaped him.

'In a way I do. I was put into foster-care after the house fire.' She didn't usually talk about that short period in her life but she suspected Caspar might understand better than most, given his own experience.

'I thought you went to your grandmother's?'

'I did, eventually. But remember I wasn't talking because of the PTSD and no one knew my gran existed so they couldn't track her down. She was living interstate so it took a few days for her to even hear about the fire and for her to come forward. By then I'd had several nights in foster-care. It was horrible.'

'What happened?'

'It was just a dreadful time. My parents had just died and I was sent to stay with strangers. It wasn't their fault. I was traumatised, I wasn't speaking and no one had the time or energy, and probably not the training back then, to deal with me. I was just thinking how lucky Kristin was to have a very different experience.'

'Yes, she was. But she also had a mother who was a drug addict who turned to prostitution and left her. Kristin was lucky but don't be fooled, she has her own demons. You were lucky in different ways. You had a mother and a grandmother who loved you.'

He was right. Annie's mother had loved her, in her own way. She may have loved Annie's father more but Annie's family had never given her up.

Annie smiled. 'It's okay, I know all that. I've

had counselling. Having a few nights in foster-care hasn't scarred me for life and probably hasn't even impacted on who I am today, it's just an experience I had that I would never want to repeat, but it's nice to hear that some children have a better time of it.'

'I think Kristin would agree with you. She and her husband are foster-parents now too. That's her cause, as you call it, so I guess it wasn't all bad for her.'

'Have you all chosen causes that resonant with each of you?'

Caspar smiled. 'I guess we have. Brig was born to an unmarried mother, although I think she was just out of her teens, and I was adopted after I was abandoned as a baby.'

'You were abandoned?' Caspar's casual tone shocked Annie. She couldn't believe he'd never mentioned this to her. They'd spent hours discussing her family yet he hadn't mentioned the fact that he was adopted as a baby. Why hadn't he said anything?

Caspar nodded.

Annie knew very well how much she had struggled to overcome feelings of abandonment after her parents' deaths, even though it had been a tragic accident. She couldn't imagine how someone dealt with being abandoned as a child.

'Have you ever had any contact with your birth parents?'

He shook his head. 'No. I have no desire to either. I have a family I love, I don't need anything more.'

'You're remarkably matter-of-fact about it.'

'I have no reason to be otherwise. I was adopted as a baby, I've only known one family. One life. My life. Although I admit I did go through a stage of wondering what my birth mother was like when I was quite young. I went through the stage of wishing I had a different family, like I think most kids do at some point, and I used to imagine what it would be like for her to come and get me, but when it dawned on me that she was probably never coming back I decided to focus on what I could control.

'Mum explained all the reasons why my birth mother might have needed to give me up without ever condemning her. I'm very grateful to my parents for the life I've had and if I can help other children and families in some way then I think I'm making an important contribution. I do feel the need to give something back.'

'And now, if you're not coming in with me, I'd better go and give Brig an update.' He leant over and kissed her softly on the lips. 'Thanks for looking after Krissy for me. I'll see you to-morrow.'

Annie watched him walking up to Brigitte's front door. If she had thought she'd had a lot of questions running through her mind before, she had twice as many now. She needed to go home and try to make sense of what she'd just learned. Did any of it matter? Did it have any impact on her? On them? She really didn't know but she needed to find out.

She'd never been through what Caspar, Brigitte and Kristin had, and it was amazing to see the people they had become thanks to the love and support they had been given. Chemistry wasn't the answer, neither was biology, but it seemed as though love could be.

Caspar's strength, resilience and humour and

his willingness to help others was encouraging. He had taken control and had shaped himself into the person he was today. He hadn't let history decide his fate. If he could do it, she could too. She was making a new life for herself and it could be anything she wanted.

Annie saw just how close Caspar's family was two days later when she made the decision to induce Kristin's baby. Kristin's blood pressure and protein levels had remained high and when the ultrasound scans of the baby looked good, Annie decided it was time to introduce the baby to the world.

The delivery was a family affair. Naturally Kristin's husband, John, was there, as was Caspar in his role as paediatrician. Brigitte had Kristin's two older children and once the baby, a little girl, was born, Brigitte brought the entire family to the hospital, including Caspar's dad.

It was such a joyful occasion and Annie knew it was going to become one of her favourite deliveries. It was a moment to be celebrated and the St Claire family was making the most of the opportunity.

'That's one thing we do well. Celebrate,' Caspar told her. 'Mum was big on celebrations. She loved celebrating anything from losing a first tooth to winning a prize at school to birthdays.'

Kristin and John named their daughter Gabriele, in memory of Kristin's foster-mother, and that gave them all cause for further celebrations. Annie liked how they talked about their mother and it was obvious she'd had a big impact on their lives. Just like the St Claire family was impacting on her life now. She now had ties, not only to Caspar but also to Brigitte through the teenage mothers' programme and to Kristin as her ob-gyn.

That concerned her a little. She could feel herself getting drawn in by his family, a little like an insect in a spiderweb, and she wondered how she was going to feel when Caspar left Mount Gambier and she lost not only him but his family too.

She wondered if she should be starting to think about how to extricate herself from Caspar's family before it was too late. But over the following week she found she had more contact with them than ever.

Whenever she popped in to see Kristin for her postnatal follow-ups there was always someone visiting her and then Caspar's father got a bed in the nursing home, which meant, because Brigitte had her hands full with minding Kristin's and John's older children, it fell to Caspar to move his father into the nursing home so he had less time for Annie. At times it felt like she was seeing more of Caspar's family then she was of him.

As she left the gym on Saturday she had a phone call from Caspar. His words echoed her thoughts.

'I feel like I've barely seen you. I'm at my dad's house. I've been going through some of his papers in his study but I need a break. You don't fancy coming over, do you? I have wine.'

Annie didn't need bribes to persuade her. She got the address and made her way to Bay Road. Caspar's father's house was towards the top of the road on the hill up to Blue Lake, not far from the Courts where he would have spent time as a lawyer. It was a magnificent house, built from local limestone with an elegant bay-windowed facade shaded by an enormous oak tree. It was obviously the St Claire family home.

Annie found Caspar sitting in the back garden, nursing a glass of red wine. She'd never known him to drink on his own and she wondered nervously if this was something he did often, but when she saw his expression she knew it was out of character. Something was bothering him.

This was her chance to listen to him. It always seemed to be her issues they were discussing and if he had a problem she wanted to be able to offer comfort for a change. A bottle of wine and an extra glass were sitting on a table beside him. She poured herself a glass, noting it was John and Kristin's label. John had already given her a dozen bottles of the same wine as a thank-you for delivering Gabriele.

Annie took her glass and perched herself on Caspar's lap. She brushed his dark hair from his forehead and kissed him gently. He put his glass down, wrapped his arms around her waist and rested his head against her shoulder.

'Thanks for coming.'

His voice was sombre and Annie hoped that whatever it was that was bothering him wouldn't be too difficult to fix.

'What's happened?' she asked.

'Nothing. The house just feels too empty. I know Dad hasn't lived here for a couple of months so nothing's really changed but it felt too lonely and sad. I needed a break and a glass of wine but I didn't want to drink alone.'

Annie suspected Caspar was also feeling bereft. Sad, like the house.

'What's going to happen to the house?'

'We're going to put it on the market. None of us need to live in it.'

'Is that what's bothering you? Selling your family home?'

'I don't know.' Caspar looked around the garden. 'This place holds a lot of happy memories for me, for all of us. I guess it is going to be hard to let it go.'

'Do you have to sell it right away? You've all got a lot to cope with at the moment.'

'What do you mean?'

'I think you're mourning. It's the end of an era.

Your dad has gone into a nursing home, his condition is not going to improve and I think you need time to come to terms with that. The father you knew has changed and perhaps now isn't the time to deal with selling the house as well. Why don't you rent it out while you get used to the changes? That might be a gentler transition. It'll give you a bit of time to get used to the idea that your father won't be coming home.'

'I guess we could look at that as an option, although it might be simpler to sell it than to get it ready to rent.'

'Can I see the house?' she asked, keen to see where he'd grown up.

'Of course.' He topped up their glasses and they wandered through the house. The rooms were large and spacious, the kitchen and bathrooms had been modernised, but there were relics of Caspar and his siblings' teenage years throughout. Annie knew he'd gone to boarding school so his strongest memories were probably all formed before the age of thirteen, and being the last house his mother had lived in would make it even harder to let go.

The house was fully furnished, which begged the question. 'Why didn't you stay here instead of in the apartment?' Annie thought he would have preferred to be in his childhood home.

'I felt a bit strange about sleeping in my parents' bed.'

'What about your own room? Or did that get turned into an en suite the minute you left for boarding school?'

'Not quite.' Caspar had one hand on a door handle. 'This was my room,' he said as he opened one of the last doors off the hallway.

Annie stepped inside, curious to see what traces of the teenage Caspar remained.

'I'm a bit too big now for a single bed,' he said.

'It looks comfy enough,' she said as she bent over and leant both hands on the mattress, giving it a couple of gentle pushes to test its firmness. 'I don't suppose this bed has ever seen any action?' she asked as she glanced back over her shoulder, thinking that perhaps she could distract him from his sombre thoughts.

Caspar shook his head.

Annie straightened up. 'It would be a shame

to let a good bed go to waste, don't you think?' she said as she stepped out of her canvas sneakers and started to unbutton her shorts.

She didn't get a chance to finish undressing. Caspar did it for her.

His old bed was narrow but they didn't need a lot of room.

CHAPTER NINE

ANNIE LAY CURLED into Caspar's side. She had one leg thrown over the top of his thigh her foot tucked against his knee as she ran her fingers in lazy circles over his bare chest. 'This is nice,' she said. 'It's like we're hidden from the world and no one would be able to find us.'

'Maybe I should keep the house and we could meet here for dirty weekends once I'm back in Melbourne,' he suggested, his earlier sombre mood dispatched by their lovemaking.

Caspar only had two weeks left but it was the first time he had mentioned leaving. She knew he was going, they both did, but that didn't mean she wanted to talk about it. They'd had enough serious discussion for one day.

'You'd have to get a bigger bed,' she said, trying to lighten the mood.

'If I did, would you stay the night?'

'Maybe.' Staying the night would make their relationship seem more serious. She'd already breached her own rules by getting involved with him, she'd well and truly let him out of the box, but while she could get him to leave her bed before morning, while she didn't wake up with him beside her, she could tell herself it was still all just a harmless bit of fun.

'I've been invited to a film premiere in Sydney next week,' he told her. 'The Park Hyatt has big beds. Would you come with me?'

He'd been trying to get her away for a weekend for a while but so far she'd managed to avoid agreeing to his suggestion. She smiled. 'Did you think you could get me in a moment of weakness?'

'It might be my only chance.'

'I can't have a weekend off. What if one of my patients goes into labour and needs me?' She rolled out one of her favoured excuses but this time he was ready with an answer.

'It's one weekend. Have you got any expectant mothers due in the next few days? Can't the local GPs cover you?' he asked. 'You're allowed to take holidays. We could leave Friday night and be back on Sunday. I want to be able to wake up beside you in the morning. I want to be able to take you out.'

'Out?'

'Yes, in public. It's Sydney, no one will take any notice of us.'

Was this her opportunity? She hated making him leave before daybreak but she couldn't risk someone seeing him leave her house in the morning or, worse, seeing them arrive together at the hospital. In Sydney, in a hotel, they could have a whole night together without compromising their privacy. But staying together overnight wasn't the only issue.

'What about at the film premiere?' she wanted to know.

'I'm only invited to make up numbers. Do you think anyone will be interested in me when it's Hugh Jackman's new movie?'

'Hugh Jackman!' Annie sat up in bed. 'Will he be there?'

'Apparently.'

'I love him.'

'So you'll come?' He was laughing now, his good humour well and truly restored.

Annie nodded. She couldn't resist. She'd get to spend the weekend with Caspar, pretending they had a proper relationship, *and* she'd get to see her favourite movie star. She couldn't say favourite celebrity any more as Caspar had that mantle. As long as they could preserve some anonymity she didn't think it could get much better.

'You have no qualms about invading his privacy, then?' Caspar asked.

'If I ran into him at the supermarket I'd leave him alone, but if he's promoting his movie, that's work for him and he would be fair game.'

Annie and Caspar woke up to a glorious Sydney morning. From their bed, which was as big as Caspar had promised, they could look across the harbour to the Opera House, where the iconic building's white sails contrasted sharply with the brilliant blue sky.

They had brunch at Bondi Beach and spent the early afternoon lying on the warm golden sand. Caspar was incognito in board shorts, a hat and sunglasses, and despite being shirtless and tanned and gorgeous nobody seemed to recognise him and nobody bothered them.

Annie tensed when she noticed a film crew setting up on the beach a short distance from where they lay until Caspar pointed out that it was a rival network preparing to film an episode for their reality TV series about lifeguards.

'I told you people don't always recognise me,' he said.

'I bet you they do in Melbourne and I know for a fact they do in Mount Gambier. No one expects to see you here, that's the difference.'

Caspar shrugged. 'My turn in the spotlight won't last long. There are always new celebrities being created in this day of reality television. You only need to look over there to see that I'm right.'

Annie glanced across to where a crowd of locals and tourists had gathered around the cameras. She laughed and relaxed, the irony of the situation not lost on either of them.

'Maybe,' she agreed, too lethargic and comfortable to argue or even think about what he was saying. The heat of the sun was soporific and she closed her eyes and caught up on some of the sleep she'd lost the night before when she and Caspar had made the most of their luxurious bed.

They returned to the hotel in time for an early dinner, before changing for the premiere. Annie had borrowed a red evening gown of Tori's and the hotel had arranged for a hairdresser to come to their room. By the time she had finished attending to Annie, Caspar was ready. He looked impossibly handsome in his black suit, crisp white shirt and bow-tie and part of Annie wished the evening was already over so she could have him to herself. But the real world waited.

Annie's stomach was churning with nerves as the limousine pulled away from the hotel and headed to the premiere. Apprehension and excitement fought for attention. She was equally apprehensive about being on public display—she knew Caspar would not go unnoticed when they arrived at the premiere, he was far too gorgeous to be unobtrusive, but she was also excited to think that she was about to experience a proper night out. But her apprehension increased disproportionately as they drew nearer to the theatre.

Camera flashes lit the night sky like fireworks and Annie's heart was racing as she saw the crush of photographers and journalists standing behind the barriers, waiting to capture a photo or grab thirty seconds to speak to a celebrity.

Caspar stepped from the limousine at the end of the red carpet and reached for her hand to help her out. Her mouth was dry and her hands were clammy.

'Are you okay?'

'Can I sneak in a back entrance?' she asked. She felt faint and a little nauseous and she wasn't certain she was going to make it anywhere.

Caspar bent his head until his lips were millimetres from her ear. 'No way. I want you with me. You look gorgeous,' he said, as his eyes travelled down the length of her gown. 'Let me show you off. Come on, it'll be fun.'

Annie wasn't so sure.

'I'll take care of you,' he said. 'I promise. It's only a few steps and we'll be inside. No one will take any notice of us.'

Despite his assurances that no one would be interested in him, she could already hear journalists clamouring for Caspar's attention and the noise and jostling reminded her of the last time she'd had the press hounding her. That time she'd been standing on the steps of a courthouse knowing she was about to lose everything. It wasn't one of her best memories.

She longed to find another way into the theatre. She desperately wanted to avoid the media, but she knew it would be next to impossible to get away now and she didn't really want to leave Caspar's side. He made her feel safe. She'd seen how he cared for his sisters and his father and his patients and she knew he would do the same for her. It was time to trust him.

She took a deep breath and gripped his hand a little more firmly, taking comfort from his strength as she stepped forward in her strappy sandals. She could hardly believe this was happening. A month ago she would never have dreamed she could brave such an event.

They'd taken three steps along the red carpet when Caspar was asked to stop for a photo. Annie tried to step out of the shot but he pulled her in close to his side as he smiled for the camera.

'And who is your date tonight, Dr St Claire?' the photographer asked as his flash temporarily blinded Annie.

'Dr Annie Simpson.'

The photographer was asking more questions but Caspar turned and kept walking. Annie was vaguely aware that the questions related to her and to their relationship but Caspar ignored him as he led Annie inside. She was glad Caspar had answered on her behalf, glad he had given just the right amount of information. She knew she would have made a mess of any reply.

Her mouth was so dry her tongue was stuck to the roof of her mouth and she was in desperate need of a glass of water. If Caspar hadn't been holding her hand she didn't think she would have made it inside. Her knees were like jelly. She couldn't believe she'd let Caspar talk her into this but if it wasn't for his strength she knew she wouldn't have made it.

He waited until they made it into the sanctuary of the theatre and away from the prying eyes of the media before he gave her a quick kiss and a wink. 'Well done,' he said, and his praise gave her enough courage to make it through the rest of the evening.

The movie was fabulous but the best was yet to come. They were invited to attend the after-party. Annie had an amazing night. She got to meet the star of the movie and his wife, who were both lovely, but the highlight was spending quality time with Caspar. It was such a pity that this wasn't anything like their real life, she thought on more than one occasion.

The only moment of concern was when they were asked to pose for another photo, this time with Gail, Caspar's producer and her partner. Annie was sure it was the same photographer who had taken their photo earlier in the evening and she couldn't understand why he would need another. But Caspar assured her that the photo would probably never be used, surely there would be plenty of other more newsworthy celebrities, and he eventually convinced her to relax by taking her onto the dance floor, where she managed to forget all about inquisitive newshounds.

She didn't notice the photographer taking a few more candid shots of her and Caspar during the evening. Neither did she notice him in deep conversation with a newspaper reporter. She wasn't aware of anything other than what a good time she was having.

She felt like Cinderella at the ball and she wished the night could last for ever. She floated around the room and at times felt that the only thing anchoring her to the floor was Caspar. It was like a dream, a glorious, colourful, delightful dream. She wanted to absorb everything about it—the music, the food, the people—and store the memories away. She was glad she'd agreed to spend the weekend with him.

It was an experience she'd never forget and she secretly wondered, if she relaxed and let go of her past and embraced the future, whether things could always be like this. While she was with Caspar she almost believed she could do it. What was the worst that could happen?

Her positive frame of mind lasted until Monday morning when they were back in Mount Gambier and she was getting ready for work when Caspar arrived at her house unexpectedly, and very early, carrying an armful of papers.

She greeted him at the kitchen door. 'Hi, what are you doing here?'

She was pleased to see him, although he didn't look quite as happy and relaxed as she was used to. Perhaps, like her, he was wishing they were back in Sydney.

'There's something you need to see,' he said as he dumped the newspapers on her kitchen table. His green eyes were dark, a sure sign that he was distracted. Either something was bothering him or he was thinking about sex. Annie doubted it was the latter, judging by his expression.

'There's no easy way to tell you this,' he continued. 'You're in the papers.'

'Me? Why?' Annie's heart plummeted, sinking like a rock to collide with her stomach. Was something she'd done to blame for Caspar's expression? He definitely looked far from happy and relaxed. Annie thought he looked ill.

'One of the journalists at the film premiere must have gone looking for a story. He found yours.'

'What?'

Annie separated the papers. Caspar had brought the Sydney, Melbourne and local papers and had folded all of them to the entertainment sections.
Annie read the first headline.

Reality TV doc's heartbreaking surprise.

Beneath that, in smaller type, it said: *'The tragic past of Caspar St Claire's girlfriend.'*
'Girlfriend!' she exclaimed.
'That's not the worst bit.'
Annie read on.

Caspar St Claire has a reputation as both a compassionate doctor and a Casanova. Never short of attractive female company, Dr St Claire has been photographed with several high-profile personalities but his latest companion, Dr Annie Simpson, seen with him in Sydney last weekend, is supposedly just a colleague...

The story was punctuated with photos of them. The photo in the centre of the page was of the two of them on the red carpet but also included was the one taken with Gail and her partner. But there were more photos too, photos Annie couldn't recall being taken, photos that showed them sharing a drink and dancing, rather intimately, and it was obvious they were more than just colleagues.

Things look to be more serious than most but Dr Simpson, an obstetrician, has a complicated history. Is she the reality TV heart-throb's latest project or has he got more than he bargained for...?

Annie continued to read.

Dr Simpson first hit the headlines seventeen years ago as a twelve-year-old when she was the sole survivor of a house fire that took the lives of both her parents. Although initially under suspicion of starting the blaze, she was later cleared of any involvement when the origin of the fire was attributed to a burning cigarette in her parents' bedroom. More recently she was in the spotlight again when

her husband was gaoled for involuntary man-
slaughter. Which brings me to the question—
what has Caspar St Claire got himself into?

Annie felt sick. She collapsed onto one of the
kitchen chairs. 'I don't believe this. Why would
they print this?'

'Is it true?'

Annie shook her head. 'It's all true, but why
would someone dig this up? This is exactly what
I wanted to get away from.'

'You were accused of starting the fire that
killed your parents?'

Annie nodded.

'Who made the accusations? The authorities?'

'No. The media.'

'Why would they do that?'

Annie took comfort from the fact that Caspar sounded prepared to come to her defence. It
wasn't something she was used to. 'They jumped
to their usual sensationalistic conclusions. Because I was the only occupant who survived, they
supposed that I started it. And because I wasn't
talking, couldn't talk because of the PTSD, they

didn't bother to get my story, they just decided that made me more guilty. Once the fire department cleared me they had to retract their accusations but once those things are out in public they never really go away, hence the reason for my dislike of the media.'

Caspar nodded and moved behind her. He stood close enough that she could feel his body heat warming her back. His arm brushed against hers as he leant over her and pointed at a paragraph in the paper. 'What about this part about your husband?'

The sense she had that he was on her side evaporated with his question. Was he going to attack her over her husband's drink-driving conviction? That hadn't been her fault.

'It's true,' she admitted. 'He had, has, a drinking problem. If he drank around me I would take the car keys to make sure he couldn't drive but one night, after we had separated, he got in the car and drove and that's when he had the accident. He hit a pedestrian. She was killed and he was gaoled for six months.'

'I meant was it true that he is your husband? I thought you were divorced.'

'Oh.' Annie wasn't surprised she'd miscon-strued his question. She was so overwhelmed she couldn't think straight. 'We're divorced now but at the time of the accident we were separated so legally he was still my husband. The journal-ist hasn't printed anything that isn't correct.'

'Did you know he was an alcoholic?'

'He didn't have a drinking problem when we met. Or I should say he didn't seem to drink more than any other uni student. But his drinking es-calated when I got accepted into my specialty and he didn't.'

'He's a doctor too?'

Annie nodded. 'We met at medical school. His parents had cut off his funds after he failed his second-year exams. He needed somewhere to live so he moved in with me after my grandmother died. I thought we were bonding over our loss of family, our loneliness, but in hindsight he was using me for free accommodation. I didn't realise at the time that he was taking advantage of me. I was too naïve. I thought we were in love and getting married seemed like a good idea. It meant I wasn't alone and it entitled us to better student subsidies, something he was keen on.

'I actually thought things were okay until he started drinking. It turns out I'd picked someone just like my father. Someone who turned to the bottle when things got tough.

'Eventually, when I realised I couldn't change things if he wasn't prepared to seek help, we separated. I couldn't let my life be dictated by his addiction. My childhood had been dictated by my mother's addiction to my father and by my father's dependence on alcohol. I couldn't spend my adult years like that too. Our marriage was already over in all but name but the accident was the final straw.

'Because I'd put my grandmother's house into our joint names when we got married I had to sell it to pay his fines and legal fees. That accident changed everything but I've been trying to move on, trying to get past it. To have it brought up all over again is exactly what I didn't want.'

Annie turned the paper over, not surprised to see that her hand was shaking. She felt nauseous and she'd seen enough. She didn't need to read what the other papers had printed.

'I'm sorry,' Caspar said. 'I had no idea about any of this.'

'No. This is my fault.' She couldn't blame Caspar. She'd put herself in this situation and she'd deliberately avoided telling him her whole sordid history. She hadn't wanted anyone in her new life to know the details but that was now a moot point. She could just imagine how quickly this information would spread around the hospital and the town.

As much as she wanted to bury her head in the sand and hide, she knew the only way to deal with it was to confront it. She pushed her chair back and stood up.

'Where are you going?'

'To work.'

'Are you sure that's wise?'

'What would you suggest?' she asked. 'I have to do my job.'

'I thought you might want to let things die down a bit first. There's bound to be someone waiting for a comment from you at the hospital.'

'Well, the sooner I start setting the record straight the better, wouldn't you agree?'

Annie picked up her bag and headed for the door.

'Can I drive you?' he asked.

'No.' She shook her head. 'If the media is waiting and we arrive together, that will only fuel the fire. I can handle this.'

She didn't want to handle it but there was nothing she could do about that now. She didn't have a choice.

Caspar was only a few moments behind her as she turned into the hospital parking. Liam had parked the television network's van in its usual spot but there was an additional van parked near the ambulance bay. The extra van belonged to the local news channel and Annie knew they were there for her. Had Liam given Caspar a heads-up? Was that why Caspar had suggested she wait? Was that why he was shadowing her?

She straightened her shoulders and marched towards the entrance. She was three paces from the doors when a microphone was thrust at her.

'Dr Simpson, can you tell us how long you've been involved with Dr St Claire and did he know about your background?'

Annie stopped and turned to face the journalist. She gave him her best cold stare. 'I am not in a relationship with Dr St Claire. That is my only comment.' She turned and let the hospital swallow her. She hoped she would be left alone to do her job.

Thwarted by Annie, the reporter turned his attention to Caspar. 'Dr St Claire, do you have anything to say?'

'No comment.'

He could think of plenty to say but not to a reporter. What he wanted to say was for Annie's ears only. He had heard her answer. What he couldn't figure out was why she was denying their relationship. It wasn't going to change the facts that had been written about her in the paper. Why wouldn't she admit they were involved? At least then he'd legitimately be able to watch her back. At least then he could tell the world he knew everything he needed to know about Annie.

He could tell the media to leave her alone. But she'd deliberately shut him out. To hear her deny their relationship upset him more than the fact she'd kept secrets from him.

He caught up to her just as she stepped into the lift. The smell of jasmine enveloped him as the doors slid closed. He shut his eyes and breathed deeply, letting her scent seep into him and calm him before he spoke. He needed to count to ten, needed to phrase his question carefully. Being frustrated wasn't going to help matters.

'Why did you deny we are involved?' he asked, hoping he sounded curious, not furious.

She looked at him as if he'd gone completely mad. 'If there's no relationship, there's no story. If they think we're together, they'll keep chasing a story.' She'd been a fool to think she could escape her past while she was involved with Caspar. A fool to think the media would leave her alone. Caspar was news and so she was news, and the only way to defuse the situation was to end their relationship.

'But I can help sort this out,' he said.

'I think you've done enough already.' The lift

doors opened and Annie stepped out. Her office was a few paces along the corridor. He followed her and she kept talking but didn't break stride. 'I should never have gone with you. I should have trusted my instincts. I should never have let you out of the box.'

'Pardon?'

Annie ushered him into her office and closed the door before she answered. 'From the moment you first smiled at me all I could think about was sharing your bed. You made me think about sex, which was something I hadn't thought about in a long time. But I had other priorities. Sex wasn't a big part of my life, I didn't need it, I didn't think I wanted it. But after I met you I couldn't think of anything else. In order to focus on my priorities I thought I'd better put you into a box in my head.

'But I couldn't stop thinking about you and once I let you hold me it became even harder. Once you kissed me it became impossible. I couldn't resist you. I let you out of the box and then I couldn't stay away.'

He took a step towards her, closing the gap that separated them, but Annie stepped back.

She held up one hand, raising a virtual barrier between them. 'I never wanted to be like my mother but it seems I am. I let myself get swept away by chemistry and that is no excuse. I saw how chemistry got my mother into trouble and I swore I would never repeat her mistakes. I can't do this any more.'

'Can't do what?' Caspar was having trouble following the conversation. He was stuck on the part where Annie had admitted she couldn't resist him.

'Us. I told you, I suck at relationships. I should have learnt my lesson. We are never going to work.'

That brought him back down to earth with a bang. Was she about to walk away? He'd never been in this kind of situation before. He was always the one who walked.

He wasn't entirely sure what he should do but he didn't want to give her up and he wasn't prepared to let her give up so easily either.

'A lot of things don't work out exactly as we'd like. That doesn't mean you stop trying. Not if you want something badly enough,' he argued.

Was she going to let the media dictate their relationship? He'd thought she was tougher than that.

'Caspar, please, what is the point? You leave at the end of the week. We always knew it was going to end some time, I'm choosing to end it now.'

She was normally serious but still quick to smile, but she wasn't smiling now. Surely there had to be more to it than the media interest. She must know it would settle eventually. The media would find something more sensational to focus on and would forget all about them.

This was all his fault. It didn't matter what she said. He'd badgered her to go away for the weekend. He'd chased her when he'd known he shouldn't, but together they could get through this. If only she would let him help.

He didn't want it to be the end. He couldn't imagine it being over. Somehow, despite himself, he had found the woman he wanted to spend the rest of his life with. His perfect woman did exist and she was standing right in front of him. He couldn't let her go now. He didn't want to be without her.

He loved her.

'No,' he said. 'We can make this work. I'm not going to let you walk away.' If he didn't tell her how he felt now, he might not get another chance. This was it. She needed to know. 'I love you.'

'You can't.'

That wasn't the response he had been expecting. 'What do you mean, I can't? I do.'

She was shaking her head. 'Everyone who loves me leaves me. My mother, my grandmother.'

'Neither of them left you intentionally. I don't think anyone has ever loved you like I do.'

'But you're leaving too, aren't you? You're going back to Melbourne.'

Was that what this was about? She didn't want to be left again? Was she planning on leaving him before he left her?

'You could come with me.'

'You're not listening to me. I am not going to repeat my mother's mistakes. She was never able to just let my father go. She followed him endlessly and I am not going to do that. I will not do that.'

'I am not your father and you are not your mother. I promise I won't let you down.'

'You can't know that. I'm trying to put my life together again. I had to do that when I was twelve and I'm doing it again now. That's enough. I don't want to do it a third time when things go wrong again.'

'You can't live your life expecting the worst. You can't hide from love.'

'I'm better on my own.'

He disagreed but he tried in vain to convince her. 'You told me once your mother loved your father. She couldn't live without him. Do you love me?'

For the first time he actually wanted to make a relationship work but Annie was resolute.

'I don't know,' she said. 'I'm not sure I know what love is.'

CHAPTER TEN

CASPAR HAD BEEN gone for three weeks, four days and fifteen hours and Annie wondered how long it would be before she would stop counting.

His last week in Mount Gambier had been horrible. The media had camped outside her house and she'd had to stay with Tori, hiding from the world. But that hadn't been the worst part. The worst part had been seeing him every day but not being with him. She'd been missing him before he'd even left. She wondered when she would stop.

Losing her mother and her grandmother had been hard but this was worse. Much worse.

Maybe it was because his absence was still so new. She felt as though he'd been taken from her life before she was ready. Perhaps if they'd had more time together she would have discovered things about him that had irritated her. Perhaps then she would have been glad to say goodbye.

She tried making a mental list of the things that had annoyed her. Maybe that would ease the pain.

He always had an answer for everything and he was usually right.

He had a terrible habit of laughing at her when she was mad.

He was stubborn.

He ignored boundaries.

She had to admit, as far as lists went, it wasn't very good. If it wasn't for those things they would never have got together. If he'd taken no for an answer or respected boundaries she would never have ended up in his arms or in his bed, and no matter how much she was hurting now she knew she didn't regret the experience. She just wished it hadn't ended so soon.

But she'd recover. Given time. It was just going to take longer than three weeks, four days and fifteen hours.

After three weeks, four days and eighteen hours Kristin arrived for her six-week postnatal check-up. Annie went through the formalities of the appointment, which included admiring the baby and asking after the rest of Kristin's family. Kristin proceeded to fill her in on the activities of her offspring but that wasn't who Annie wanted to hear about. However, as she didn't want to be the one to bring up the topic of Caspar she had to wait patiently until Kristin, hopefully, got around to it.

'You haven't forgotten about Gabriele's baptism, have you?' Kristin asked. 'This Sunday, at St Paul's.'

Annie had been pleased to be invited to the baby's baptism and she hadn't forgotten. She was looking forward to having a reason to go out. 'Eleven o'clock, right?'

Kristin nodded. 'Caspar is coming home for it. Did you know?'

Annie felt the colour drain from her face. She shook her head. 'I haven't heard from him.' Hearing that he was coming to the Mount and hadn't bothered to let her know was almost more than she could bear. Did he know she had been invited to the baptism? Was he going to turn up and act as if nothing had happened? Annie knew she had called off their relationship, there had been no other option, but she hadn't realised how much it was going to hurt.

'Not at all?'

'Judging by the papers and magazines, he's been far too busy to stay in touch with me.' On more than one occasion over the past few weeks Annie had seen photographs of Caspar out with different women. At times it seemed like he had a different companion every night.

Kristin didn't ask for clarification, she seemed to know exactly what Annie was talking about. 'It's not serious with any of them.'

'Not yet.'

Kristin was watching her carefully. 'You could put an end to it, you know.'

'How?'

'You could go to Melbourne.'

That wasn't an option. She wasn't going to be like her mother. She wasn't going to run after any man, no matter how much she loved him.

The colour flooded back into Annie's cheeks. No. She couldn't love him. She loved things about him but that didn't mean she loved him.

She was confusing chemistry with love. Just like her mother. She was a fool.

'He's a good man, Annie, he'd look after you if you'd let him.'

She didn't know if Kristin was right.

She didn't know what to do.

She'd never been in love before.

Throughout Friday Annie had one eye on the door and one hand on her phone. She had no idea when Caspar was arriving in town or, for that matter, whether he'd get in touch, but she hated to think she might miss him. By Saturday afternoon she was a wreck, filled with nervous anticipation. In an attempt to calm her nerves she went straight to the gym after her morning rounds, showering before she left for home just in case she ran into him. She wanted to see him, she wanted to see if she could make sense of her feelings.

As she turned into her street, she spied a silver Audi sports car parked outside her house.

He was here. Really here.

Her hands were shaking as she negotiated the

driveway and parked under the carport at the rear of the house. Caspar was sitting on her back veranda. He stood as she switched off the engine and crossed the back lawn. Her heart hammered in her chest as she watched him in her rear-vision mirror. Her breath came in shallow spurts and she was afraid to take a deep breath, afraid if she concentrated on anything except him he might disappear.

He was divine.

She stepped out of her car on wobbly legs. She had to hold onto the door for support.

He'd had his hair cut. His dark curls were shorter but his green eyes were just the same, hypnotic, mesmerising. She was scared to ask what he was doing there. Why he'd come. She was afraid the answer might not be the one she wanted to hear.

He'd almost reached her. She waited for him to speak first. She didn't trust her voice.

'I was beginning to think I was waiting at the wrong house.'

A sense of relief flooded through her. Nothing had changed. He still managed to surprise her.

She laughed and her nervousness eased. 'Of all the things I thought you might say, that wasn't on my list.'

'What was?' he asked.

'I thought you might tell me you've missed me. That you've been miserable without me.'

'Would you like me to be miserable?' He smiled, looking far from despondent, and Annie's stomach flip-flopped at the sight of his familiar grin.

'A bit,' she admitted. 'Just so you'd know how I've been feeling.'

'Oh, Annie, of course I've missed you.' He closed the gap between them and Annie stepped towards him, meeting him halfway. He wrapped his arms around her and she rested her head over his heart, letting its rhythm calm her nerves further as she breathed in his peppermint scent. 'Why do you think I'm here?'

'For Gabriele's baptism.'

'No, not in the Mount, *here* here.' He kept one arm wrapped around her as he stroked her hair with his other hand. 'I wanted to see you.'

That was the answer she'd been hoping for

but it wasn't enough information. 'How long are you staying?' Her voice was muffled against his chest. How long would they have before he left again? An hour, a night, two?

'That depends.'

'On?'

He took her hand and led her to the chair on the veranda. He sat in the chair and pulled her onto his knee. She didn't resist. She was right where she wanted to be.

'On whether I can get a job here.'

Annie frowned. 'Here? But what about your job in Melbourne? What about the television series?'

'I've resigned,' he told her. 'From the hospital and from the show. You know that Phil has decided, after his long-service leave, to resign from his position as paediatrician.' Annie nodded, she'd heard the news. 'I've applied for his job. I don't want to be in Melbourne. I want to be here.'

He was returning to the Mount? 'Why?'

'This is my home, but it wasn't until we put my parents' house on the market that I realised what I was about to lose. You understand that, you experienced it when you sold your grandmother's house, but until now I've never missed a place to call home because home was always here, even if I chose to live elsewhere. But now I've realised I don't want to give it up.'

'The house?'

He nodded. 'I had a meeting with Dad, his lawyers and the real estate agent this morning. I've spoken to my sisters and I've bought the house. I'm coming home.'

He'd bought the house. He was coming back to live. Annie wasn't sure exactly what that meant. Could they start again? Did he want to?

'I did a lot of thinking about our situation and I realised it was unfair of me to expect you to move for me when I wasn't offering you what you wanted. I know you want security and I want to give that to you. Despite the fact that I am currently unemployed and temporarily homeless...' he grinned '...I want to share my life with you. I want to give you the house as a wedding present.'

'What?' Annie wasn't sure she was following the conversation.

'A wedding present,' he repeated. 'I want to

put the house in your name. It's your security,'
he said as he lifted her off his lap and put her on
the chair. He got down on one knee and held her
hands in his.

'People talk about soul mates, about their other
halves, but I never really expected to be lucky
enough to find the person I wanted to spend the
rest of my life with until I met you.' He looked
up at her, his green eyes luminous.

'Until I met you I couldn't imagine believing
in, trusting enough in another person to make
that commitment. But I know you are my other
half. I know I won't find anyone else like you. I
don't even want to look. I love you, Annie. Will
you marry me?'

'You want to marry me?'

He nodded. 'I thought I'd had my happy ending. I thought I was lucky to have been given the
family I have, the family who chose me, but now
I'm getting greedy. I want you to choose me too.
I want another happy ending. With you. I want
you to marry me.'

Annie couldn't think straight. He wanted to

marry her. He'd bought her a house. He loved her. 'I feel like I should have some objections.'

Caspar laughed. 'I'd be disappointed if you didn't—you've never agreed with me without some sort of debate first. But I have known you to change your mind before and fortunately I know how to convince you. Just give me a minute,' he said as he stood up, 'I'm too old to stay down on my knees, waiting for you to come to a decision.'

He pulled her up off the chair and took her place, putting her back on his lap. He wrapped an arm around her waist, sliding his hand under the hem of her top and resting it against her hip. His hand was warm and his touch lit a fire in her belly. 'Okay, let's hear your objections.'

'I'm no good at relationships.' That was the first one.

'We have the rest of our lives to get it right,' he said as he kissed the side of her neck. 'Next.'

'I've been married before and it didn't work out so well.'

'What can I say? You married the wrong guy.' His lips moved up her neck and he kissed her just below her ear. The fire in her belly spread to her groin and she struggled to remember what she'd been about to say.

'I'm afraid of being like my mother. She would have been better off on her own.'

'I think we're better off together than apart and you don't need to chase me, I'm not running anywhere. I'm right here. From what you've told me, your parents' relationship was nothing like ours. Your mother talked about being less miserable when she was with your father. Did she ever talk about being happy?'

Annie shook her head.

'Do I make you happy?' he asked, as his hand slid up inside her shirt and found her breast.

'Yes.' Her voice was breathless with longing.

'Well, then, are you going to make me ask twice? As usual?' His fingers were caressing her nipple. Annie could feel it peaking under his touch. 'Will you please marry me?'

'I'm afraid of making a bad decision,' she said, although she didn't think she was actually capable of making any decision, good or bad, right at that moment.

'I promise that marrying me will be the best decision of your life. We belong together. We are going to have a long and happy life together. With our own family.'

'You want children?'

'Of course. But only if you are their mother. We should be parents, don't you think—an ob-gyn and a baby doctor? We're meant to be parents. So, you see, you can have as many objections as you like and I will find a way around them. For every objection you have I will have a dozen reasons why we should get married, but there are only two that really matter. One—I love you. Two—I think you love me. Am I right?'

Could he be right? He seemed so sure, so confident.

She wanted to believe him.

It all depended on love. Could she do this? Could she depend on love?

It was up to her.

He was offering her everything she wanted. It was up to her to take it.

Chemistry wasn't the answer. Biology wasn't the answer. Was love the answer?

She could put the past behind her and have a new beginning with the man she loved.

It was up to her.

She nodded and his smile was enough to convince her she was making the right choice. 'Yes. I do love you. Even unemployed and homeless, I still love you. I will always love you.'

'And you will marry me?'

She was grinning like an idiot too now. 'Yes, I will marry you.'

'And have my babies?'

'Yes to that too,' she said. 'Should we go inside and practise?'

'That sounds like a very good idea to me.'

Annie put her hands up to his face and turned it towards her. She kissed him, a deep, searching kiss that was filled with love. She took him into her heart and then she took him to her bed.

* * * * *

Mills & Boon® Large Print
Medical

March

April

May

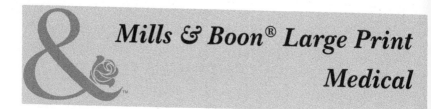

Mills & Boon® *Large Print*
Medical

June

FROM VENICE WITH LOVE
CHRISTMAS WITH HER EX
AFTER THE CHRISTMAS PARTY…
HER MISTLETOE WISH
DATE WITH A SURGEON PRINCE
ONCE UPON A CHRISTMAS NIGHT…

Alison Roberts
Fiona McArthur
Janice Lynn
Lucy Clark
Meredith Webber
Annie Claydon

July

HER HARD TO RESIST HUSBAND
THE REBEL DOC WHO STOLE HER HEART
FROM DUTY TO DADDY
CHANGED BY HIS SON'S SMILE
MR RIGHT ALL ALONG
HER MIRACLE TWINS

Tina Beckett
Susan Carlisle
Sue MacKay
Robin Gianna
Jennifer Taylor
Margaret Barker

August

TEMPTED BY DR MORALES
THE ACCIDENTAL ROMEO
THE HONOURABLE ARMY DOC
A DOCTOR TO REMEMBER
MELTING THE ICE QUEEN'S HEART
RESISTING HER EX'S TOUCH

Carol Marinelli
Carol Marinelli
Emily Forbes
Joanna Neil
Amy Ruttan
Amber McKenzie